# 2001

# AN ODYSSEY
# IN WORDS

# 2001

# AN ODYSSEY
# IN WORDS

Commemorating the Centenary of
Sir Arthur C. Clarke's Birth

Edited by
## Ian Whates and Tom Hunter

NewCon Press
England

First edition, published in the UK July 2018 by NewCon Press

NCP 151 (hardback), NCP 152 (softback)

10 9 8 7 6 5 4 3 2 1

ISBN: 978-1-910935-75-0 (hardback)
978-1-910935-76-7 (softback)

Cover art by Fangorn
Final text layout by Storm Constantine

# Contents

Editors' Dedication:

To truly appreciate the future, one must first honour the past

The editors would like to dedicate this book to the memories of Constance Ellin, Christine Havelock, Margot Whates, Bill Whates and, of course, Sir Arthur C. Clarke.

# Introduction

Tom Hunter, the Awards Director of the Arthur C. Clarke Award, and I came up with the idea of *2001: An Odyssey In Words* over a few drinks, which I'm sure will come as a great surprise to anyone who knows us (ahem…). Tom mentioned that he would like to do something special to commemorate the centenary of Sir Arthur's birth and, since books are what NewCon does, it seemed a natural avenue to explore.

NewCon Press had previously worked with the Clarke Award in 2011, producing *Fables from the Fountain* as homage to one of my favourite of Sir Arthur's collections, *Tales from the White Hart.* That book proved a lot of fun to do and I relished the prospect of putting together a second volume linked with the Award. This time, though, would be a little different. We wanted to pay tribute to another classic Clarke title but in an unexpected way; rather than setting contributors the challenge of writing within a 'shared world' setting as I had with *Fables,* this time they would have the freedom to write whatever they wanted, so long as it was science fiction; they merely had to do so in precisely 2001 words.

The suggestion was Tom's. I'm not sure how seriously he meant it, but I seized upon the idea immediately, convinced that it was a good one. Thankfully, many writers seemed to agree. When we approached past winners of the Clarke Award and those who had been shortlisted, the response was far better than we could ever have hoped for, with authors inspired by the challenge rather than daunted by it. Even given the pedigree of the writers we were approaching, the quality of submissions we received delighted us, particularly given the constraints.

One aspect did defeat us, however: our initial aim had been to release the book on the centenary of Sir Arthur's birth, December 16th 2017. It soon became clear that this would be unachievable, and we were both determined to get this right rather than rush out something that was sub-standard in order to meet a deadline.

Our thanks go out to everyone who has been involved in this

project, especially the authors who have risen to the challenge and delivered such fabulous work, both fiction and non-fiction, and to everyone who supported the Kickstarter and ensured the book is everything we hoped it would be, to Fangorn for producing such a superb cover image, and to all those attendees of Innominate, the 2017 Eastercon (the annual British national SF convention), who entered our *2001: The SFactor* competition to win a place in the anthology (won against strong competition by Allen Stroud). Last but not least, thanks to you, the reader. We hope you enjoy the stories that follow as much as we have.

*Ian Whates*
*Cambridgeshire*
*May 2018*

# Golgotha

## Dave Hutchinson

"Tell me, Father," said the Lupo cleric as we walked along the beach, "do you think of yourself as a religious man?"

I thought about that for a while, conscious of the cameras and long-distance mikes behind us. Finally, I said, "That seems an... unusual question, if you don't mind my saying so. Considering my profession. Considering *our* profession."

"You present as a man of faith," the Lupo said.

"I am, although my faith has been tested many times."

"There is no such thing as faith, unless it has been tested."

I glanced over my shoulder at the crowd we had left behind up the beach. I couldn't see the Bishop among the newsmen and politicians and soldiers, but I knew he was there, probably sheltering from the wind and having a sneaky cigarette while the world's attention was on me and the alien.

"Your faith teaches that everyone is a child of God," the Lupo said, the great clawed feet of its environment suit crunching the shingle as it walked. "I would beg to differ. I do not consider myself a child of your God, nor you a child of mine."

This was almost precisely the line of conversation which the Bishop had warned me against becoming involved in, "I think this is a discussion best left to our superiors," I said in what I hoped was a diplomatic tone of voice. The tone of voice was for the cameras; I doubted the Lupo would be able to tell one way or another.

The Lupo had been on Earth for almost two years now, and their every action was still world news. They were an aquatic people, if one could call creatures which swam in seas of liquid methane on the moon of a gas giant orbiting a star fifty-eight light years away *aquatic*. Everyone was familiar with their image from news broadcasts from their orbiting mother-ship, but they needed to wear heavily armoured suits to walk on the surface of our world. It had seemed absurd to

9

hope that I would one day meet one, and yet here we were.

"They're sly beggars," the Bishop had told me last week. "This one says it's a priest and it wants to see Blackfin. The Church is still formulating a position towards the Lupo, so you're not to discuss doctrinal matters with it. And Donal, don't fuck up, whatever you do."

There had been no explanation why I, and not some more senior churchman – the Bishop himself, perhaps – had to take responsibility for the visit, although I suspected the danger of *fucking up* made this little stroll a potato too hot for my superiors to carry. I was expendable, and to an extent deniable.

"I am a simple priest," I said.

"Are we not all simple priests?" the alien asked.

"Well, no," I said. Although as far as I understood it, in the Lupo religion everyone *was* a priest to a greater or lesser degree. "Some of us are simpler than others," I added, and instantly regretted the attempt at humour. The Lupo, so far as anyone could judge, *had* no sense of humour. They at least had that in common with my Bishop.

It was a chill day, and the breeze off the Atlantic made it even colder, but here beside the Lupo I felt warm, almost toasty. The radiator fins of its suit made it feel as if I stood beside a powerful patio heater. Over the past day or so, ahead of the Lupo's visit, I had been subjected to briefings by scientists and intelligence officers and at least one American General, but it was all jumbled up in my head and I was still unable to fathom how the body chemistry of a sentient being could function at those temperatures and pressures.

"They are not like us at *all*," the General had told me. "That's what you have to keep in mind, Father. Show it the fish, keep the conversation to generalities, and get it the hell out of there as soon as it's practical to do so."

In truth, I had grown a little weary of being told what to do. Ten months ago, I had been the priest of a tiny and mostly-overlooked parish. My congregation was dwindling, the younger members fleeing to the cities, the older ones dying. My biggest concern was how I was going to pay to repair the damage the previous winter's storms had done to the church roof. I felt as if I were on the edge of the world; no one cared what I thought or did. And then, everything had changed. One should always beware what one wishes for.

The cleric and I reached the water's edge. I stopped, the surf foaming around my wellingtons, but the alien walked on until it was knee-deep in the surging waves. It was almost as tall as I was, like a child's sketch of a large dog rendered in grey alloy, the double row of radiator fins on either side of its spine like the plates along the back of a stegosaurus. Its head was a ball studded with what were presumed to be audiovisual sensors, and it scanned from side to side constantly.

We looked out to sea, the alien and I, in the direction of America, and there was nothing to see, from surf to horizon. All shipping was being held back beyond a fifty-mile exclusion zone.

"Well," I said. "Looks as if we're unlucky today." Which was, deep down, what I had been hoping for.

The Lupo didn't reply. It raised its head, and from the speakers built into its chest came a rapid series of high-pitched squeaks and clicks, loud enough to hurt my eardrums. I took a few steps back, looked behind me, but no one in the crowd was moving. There were several news channels devoted to the Lupo, their doings on Earth, and the strictly-rationed details about themselves. These channels had hundreds of millions of viewers, and it occurred to me that every one of them was watching me, paddling in the Atlantic beside a creature born tens of light years from our solar system. That was why no one was joining us; nobody wanted to be in shot if things went tits-up.

The Lupo stopped emitting the sounds, and the last of them seemed to echo and banner in the wind before fading away to nothing. Then the alien seemed to wait. It broadcast the noises again, and again waited. Then a third time, and this time, out beyond the breakers, I saw a distinctive black fin break the surface, disappear, reappear a little nearer to shore, and then begin to move back and forth. It was hardly an unusual sight, but even now I felt a little thrill.

Blackfin had been found washed up on the beach last year, severely wounded, possibly by the propeller of one of the boats that took tourists on trips around the bay. Volunteers had come from all over Ireland to try and save the stricken dolphin, but she died, and researchers from Dublin had taken her body away for study.

A few days later, as they prepared to perform an autopsy, Blackfin was seen to stir and then shudder, and then take a shaky but deep breath. The researchers rushed her to a tank, where over the following days she made a full recovery.

In time, after the astonished scientists had completed their tests, Blackfin had been released back into the wild, and a month or so ago she had been spotted in the bay. The Miracle Dolphin had become quite a tourist attraction; the hotels and guest houses in the village were booked up for well over a year in advance, and for the first time in several years my congregation had begun to grow again.

It had been quietly suggested that, as the local priest, I take no position on Blackfin; the Christian parallels were far too stark and obvious, and the Church, already struggling with the question of the Lupo and their God, were not yet minded to confront the concept of a cetacean Messiah. God had seen fit, in His mysterious way, to deliver one of His creatures. That's the official line, Donal. Oh, and by the way, don't fuck up.

The Lupo broadcast its noises once more, and this time Blackfin broke the surface and I heard, faint and far away and broken by the wind, the sound of the dolphin *answering*, and I felt a line of cold trace its way down the centre of my back.

The alien's suit must have amplified the sound from the ocean; I could barely hear it over the wind and the waves but the Lupo spoke again, another series of clicks and whistles, and the dolphin replied once more. They were, I realised, having a *conversation*.

The conversation went on for some time. I looked back, but no one in the crowd seemed at all alarmed at this turn of events, and I realised they simply could not hear it. They were too far away, there was too much ambient noise. I was the only witness. That was why I was there, of course. Not because I was a trustworthy local but because I was God's representative on this bleak beach in the West of Ireland, the place where Blackfin had died. I was there to bear witness. I looked at the alien and suddenly felt very afraid. Mankind's record, when it came to the creatures of the ocean, was not terribly noble.

By the time I realised all this, of course, it was far too late. It had already been too late when the Lupo first set foot on the beach. I could not understand what the Lupo and Blackfin were saying, but I knew in my heart what they were discussing. They were talking about *us*, and our millennia-long despoilation of the seas, and all I could do was stand there helplessly.

Abruptly, the conversation ended. The Lupo fell silent, and the dolphin slipped out of sight beneath the waves. The alien didn't move; it just stood there silently, the sea-foam rushing around its legs.

"So, Father," the Lupo said finally. "If this is a miracle, *whose* miracle is it?"

I opened my mouth to speak, but no sound came out.

"There is the God of those who walk and the God of those who fly and the God of those who swim," the alien went on, and this time I heard a noise from behind me, shouting, and I thought perhaps someone in the crowd had finally worked out what was going on. "It is strange to me that the God of those who swim has chosen to show Her benediction on this world, but one does not, after all, question the word of God, does one, Father?" The Lupo had not wanted to marvel at the Miracle Dolphin; it had come to *commune*, to *worship*. It had come to receive *Gospel*.

The Lupo were a spacefaring race, as far advanced from us as the *Conquistadores* had been from the peoples of South America. We did not know what they were capable of, but it was assumed they had weapons beyond our comprehension. Much of our dealings with them had involved trying very, very hard not to anger them, and now, with a simple act of tourism – after all, what could be more harmless than looking at a dolphin? – we had undone all that.

I looked behind me. People were running down the beach towards us, but it was already far too late. Blackfin had passed on the Word of the Lupo God, and I doubted it was a message of peace and love and understanding. Blackfin had told them what we had done to the sea and its creatures.

I had not only *fucked up*; I had a terrible feeling that I had witnessed the beginning of a Crusade.

# The Monoliths of Mars

## Paul McAuley

Monoliths are scattered everywhere amongst the dwarf planets, moons, asteroids and kobolds of the solar system. And two centuries after the first were set in place, their numbers continue to multiply. Some are manufactured in licensed workshops on Earth's Moon, Vesta, Callisto and Iapetus, others by individuals or small crews, but all are cast in glossy black fullerene to the sacred ratio 1:4:9, each contains the antique circuitry that transmits a radio burst towards the heart of the galaxy when the face of a monolith is touched, and those who set them in place honour the creed that their locations are not advertised or broadcast but are secrets to be discovered.

So there are always more monoliths to be found, but apart from a solitary specimen on the tawny plains of Serengeti in my homeland of Kenya, Earth, and an unconfirmed rumour of a giant example afloat deep in Jupiter's storms, Mars is the only planet where they have been planted in any number. Most are in the northern hemisphere because the centre of the Milky Way isn't ever visible from the south; even so, you will have to cover a great deal of territory should you wish to visit them all. I hope this short guide based on my experiences will be of some help.

Despite two centuries of speculation and investigation, the motivations of those who made the first monoliths remain unclear – we don't even know their names – but many believe that the originals were intended to symbolise the universal hope that, after the Quiet War, the peoples of the solar system could unite and move forward in common harmony. There's no better example of this than the specimen erected by the founders at the centre of the fresh impact crater in Ares Valley, where the first Martian settlement stood before the nations of Earth took their revenge on bellicose pioneers who, years before the Quiet War, attempted to mount an attack on the home planet. This venerable monolith was left untouched when the Martian capital New Old Burroughs was built on the smashed ruins; now, crowning a grassy knoll in Prospect Park, it is the starting point for those who have taken a vow to visit all the monoliths of the red planet. There is usually a line of pilgrims, tourists and locals waiting to commune with it. I recommend that you first take instruction from one of the attendant contemplatives, who, for a small exchange of credit and karma, will tailor a personal mantra that will help you to focus your mind when it is your turn to place your palm against the face of the monolith and add to its tally of radio bursts.

New Old Burroughs is the nexus of the planet's railway network. From there, pilgrims must decide whether they want to travel east or west on their quest. I chose to go east, visiting in quick succession a crater in densely cratered Arabia Terra, where a second-issue monolith is elevated on a pediment above a field of gypsum dunes, the gardened bowl of a smaller crater less than a hundred kilometres away where another second-issue monolith stands amongst a knee-high forest of mosses and dwarf birches, and a new monolith in the industrial quarter of Big Rock.

From there, a long train ride will take you to the copper-mining settlement of Oracle, where you can hire a rover and drive north and east to the shore of Isidis Planitia, and a monolith that stands at the tip of a narrow peninsula jutting into the ice-choked gulf which in a couple of centuries, if the terraforming project continues at its projected pace, will become part of the Great Northern Ocean. It's best to visit at sunset. Black rocks, white ice, the pink sky turning blue as the sun drops towards the horizon, the monolith silhouetted against the sunset as you climb towards it. Even those who, like myself, were born planetside, marvel at the vast inhuman beauty of the vista as the light of the setting sun spreads along the curve of the frozen sea's horizon, and night falls and twinkling stars emerge in night's inverted bowl. The stardust river of the Milky Way pours across the sky, and to the north the Teapot Asterism guides you to the constellation of Sagittarius and the Galactic Centre. Standing in the cold, dark, silent night, touching the monolith and looking towards the destination of the signal you've triggered, is a moment of pure sublimity.

When you return to Oracle, dear reader, do not make my mistake and fall for the lies of a woman who claims to be a guide and offers to escort you safely to the disputed territory of Cerebrus Fossa, where the only other monolith set on Mars by the founders stands near the edge of one of the fractured canyons that cut across the windy lava plain. I never saw that monolith, for I was betrayed by my so-called guide to the bandits – proud fierce descendants of dispossessed first settlers – who claim the region. After many trials and tribulations (incarceration in a variety of underground redoubts while my captors tried to ransom me; a failed escape attempt; a fierce firefight with federal police), I was rescued, tried for taking part in a raid on a train, barely avoided deportation after I was exonerated, and accepted the generous offer of shelter and recuperation in the contemplative ashram at Zero Point. There, in the lowest part of Hellas Basin, the lowest point on the Martian surface, a henge of monoliths stands in a meadow circled by the deep pine forest, and a huge specimen, the biggest known, rears above the humble whitewashed buildings of the ashram.

Since they are located in the southern hemisphere, the signals of these monoliths must be piped to a transmitter in the north, but terraformed Zero Point is an idyllic spot, with an atmospheric pressure half of Earth's and an average temperature above water's freezing point, and forests and farms patchworked around chains of lakes. After many hours meditating in that henge, wearing only a rebreather and a breechclout, and many more taking instruction from contemplative scholars, I was healed in body and soul. Head shaven, dressed in the yellow robes of an initiate, I was dispatched to Olympus Mons to complete my instruction.

With tourists and ordinary pilgrims, I rode the elevator up the face of the vast cliffs at the edge of the great shield volcano to the terminus of the railway that winds up the north-western flank. The journey takes two days, plunging through passes cut in wrinkle ridges, skirting steep scarps, slumped cliffs and rare impact craters, climbing through long gullies and ravines whose walls close out all but a narrow strip of sky, and crossing endless aprons of frozen lava and fields of pumice like an ant creeping up the flanks of one of the great pyramids of Egypt.

The central spines of the carriages, studded on either side with sleep pods, became a long common space where the passengers held parties and song fests, organised yoga classes and meditation and discussion groups. I was travelling with two other initiates, and we did our best to answer questions and lead discussion and meditation sessions, and in every spare moment I found a quiet corner by a window where I could watch empty slopes still dusted primordial red (for no rain had yet fallen there) crawl past as the day sky darkened and behind and below us the flank of the mountain fell away towards the rim of the planet.

At last we disembarked at Olympus Ashram, a sealed ten-storey building rivetted into the crest of an arc of sheer cliffs at the southern side of the caldera. There, twenty-two kilometres above the rest of the planet, you can look out across the volcano's great caldera, formed from half a dozen overlapping and intersecting circles and segments of coalesced collapse craters where lava once flowed from deep magma chambers and might yet flow again, for the last eruption occurred just ten million years ago, an eye-blink of geological time. There have been quakes, up there, lofting curtains of fines from lakes of silky dust, and plumes of steam have been spotted wafting from certain of the fractures which cut across the smooth lava floor.

At the foot of the cliffs, directly below the ashram, is the beginning of a white road that arrows north across the caldera's ochre floor, but it is not the road to the monolith, for that stands eighteen kilometres to the north, at the highest point of Olympus Mons. Dressed in pressure suits, pilgrims and tourists ride there on a tram which terminates at a long ridge that curves across slopes of bare smooth lava. They disembark and, shepherded by contemplative guides, follow a path along the crest of the ridge, climbing steadily towards the rim of the sky. At last, the monolith appears, standing on a squat column or core of slightly harder basaltic lava that remained when the outer layers collapsed. The highest point on the tallest mountain on Mars.

The pilgrim path winds through an apron of debris, half-buried in the fine ochre dust that everywhere coats the peak of the volcano, to the base of the column. One by one, under an indigo sky with a few day stars visible, the visitors climb steps cut into the column and briefly commune with the monolith before reaching out and placing their gloved palm against its face. When my civilian companions on the train made this visit I was not amongst them, for I first had to spend a Martian year serving my apprenticeship. Many hours of contemplation and meditation, many more listening to the teachings of sages, work on the lamasery's maintenance crew and in the visitors' canteen, and a hundred days of solitude out in the caldera, living in a pod scarcely bigger than the first ships to sail Earth's Moon, sampling windblown dust, supervising machines that are drilling down towards the volcano's deep heart, and maintaining meteorology stations (for although the atmosphere is still vanishingly thin there is weather up there; sometimes the caldera's basin is filled with a restless fog of high-altitude orthographic clouds).

We are a scientific order.

It's true that the monoliths are patterned on those featured in a fantasy of alien intervention made at the dawn of space travel. And even though a violent campaign was once waged against them by a group who feared that they would attract our nemesis it's also true that their signals are too faint to reach the nearest stars, let alone the galactic centre. It doesn't matter. Pilgrimage to the monoliths is an act of faith and grace. A humbling affirmation of one's place in the enormity of creation. The universe's vast size and age makes possible our improbable genesis, but those vast gulfs of time and space are also our quarantine. We call out with our weak voices in the hope that one day we will be heard by others like us. We know that it is unlikely we will be answered, yet we continue to call.

I thought of this and much else when I was at last allowed to make my own pilgrimage to the highest point on Mars. I spent a day and a night in solitary meditation before I communed with the monolith, and returned to the ashram, and then to the world below.

The order sent me to Old New Burroughs. The monolith in Prospect Park. And so my journey took me all around the planet, from its lowest point to its highest and back again. Should you ever visit Mars, reader, seek me out and share your own story.

Afterwards, for a small fee, I will give you a mantra that will help you achieve a state of grace before you set your palm against the cool polished black face of the monolith, and reach out to the universe.

# Murmuration

## Jane Rogers

I've still got another month to work in the quarantine block, plus my own week in isolation. So I'm recording this here and now before I forget any details. I could tell Mitch, I guess. But what would be the point? None of us have comms with outside; quarantine is quarantine, for pathogens *and* info. And maybe I'm wrong. Christ, I hope I am wrong.

Okay. Two ships came in this week, so we have sixteen souls in quarantine. *Endeavour Astra* is back from her pre-colonising visit to Edena, 20 light years distant. Her crew are intact and healthy. The Captain sits with his earphones in while I run my tests, occasionally opening his eyes to glare as if I were an irritating insect. But Ojo their medic is friendly; curious about the new biotronic tests we've started running, and happy to chat about their mission. He's a big man with a massive hibernation beard which he's insisting on keeping, like a badge of honour. I've tried explaining that only real saddos wear them now – well, he'll see soon enough, when he gets out of here.

'It's a jewel of a planet,' he told me. 'Beautiful. Water, vegetation, temperate climate, gravity just over half of Earth's – we could settle there tomorrow.'

'Life forms?' I asked, as the Bot took his samples.

'Nothing to worry about. A few aquatic species, all edible, and small vertebrates. Nothing bigger than a rabbit.'

'So if you all come up squeaky clean after screening –'

'We will. I tested daily for pathogens. It's a virgin. There's no pollution and no contamination.'

'That's fantastic.'

'Yeah. I'm going to recommend my grandchildren to get their names down right away.'

'You have grandchildren?'

'I bloody well hope so!'

He hasn't tried to find out and I like that. Some of them, once they've been woken for re-entry, go straight into family updates. And the news is always mixed, there are always deaths and divorces as well as the births. Time won't stand still for 24 years, will it? Then they're grieving and celebrating all at once when they need to be focussing on re-entry. Better to find out naturally, once they're home, in my opinion.

Anyway, it sounded like Edena was a pretty sweet spot. 'No carnivores?' I asked him.

'Only insects. Clouds of – I dunno what you'd call them, a kind of cross between a mosquito and a bee. Blood suckers, obviously. They came swarming all round us when we landed but we sorted them out fast with Bti.'

'You sprayed? Is that allowed?'

'Sure. They were all over us. Bti's non-toxic to other organisms. Once we'd done a proper recce, Josie and Sam took the backpacks and sprayed the whole area. With any luck we've eradicated them. There are no birds, so they weren't part of a food chain.'

I nodded. A colony planet is what we've all been praying for. We are sick; sick of living underground, sick of artificial light, hungry for the sight of sky.

The second ship coming in was a different matter. No one expected her, there have been no comms in living memory. *Karellen*, one of that old Space Explorer fleet sent out in the late 21st century. She's been out there fifty years! It's a miracle she made it back. Various systems failed and four of the crew never woke up. The six who have come to us are not in good shape; radiation sickness, malnutrition, muscle wastage. A few other contaminations showed up in screening but nothing major. The captain, Helena, is a tall broad-shouldered woman with a quick smile and worryingly poor co-ordination. She needs help eating and drinking and I'm glad to do that because she is so grateful and friendly. They've been to the southern circumpolar constellation of Pavo to explore the five planets of Delta Pavonis. A couple of those are reckoned to be in the Habitable Zone.

'We were collecting specimens – which as you know mostly

means rocks – but Delta Pavonis D really is like a mini-Earth, with a proper eco-system.'

'Did you find intelligent life?'

'We did!' She laughed. 'But in a very non-human form.'

'Go on.'

'If you promise it won't go any further than this room. I haven't had my debrief yet.'

My turn to laugh. 'I'm trapped here for the next five weeks – the medics are in quarantine too, you know. Even if I wanted to spill confidential data, there's no signal in here.'

'So I'll be out before you.'

'All being well.'

'That's good to know. I don't suppose there's any fruit?'

'Sorry. Would you like some of the yoghourt stuff?'

She pulled a face but nodded, and after I'd fed her a few spoonfuls she resumed her story. 'We stayed on Delta Pavonis D a long time. We had technical problems. Our solar generator was only functioning intermittently and while it was taken apart we needed planet-grown nutrition. There was something wrong with the fuel delivery system as well, and our engineer Chris was completely baffled. The climate is temperate and cultivation was straightforward, but the more we explored and tested the more we realised that the planet itself was alive with nutritious flora and fauna. If we *had* to be stranded, it was about the best place in the galaxy to end up.'

'Water? Sunlight?' I slipped in a couple more spoonfuls.

She nodded. 'And no predators. It was as if the place was being farmed.'

'Ah, your intelligent life.'

'Uh-huh. Patty our linguist –' Her face puckered. 'Shit. She didn't wake up, did she? Oh Patty.' She shook her head and I handed her a tissue but her fingers couldn't grip. She smeared her balled fist across her eyes. 'She's the best. Was. The best, ever. She was the one who cracked it.'

It was time for my own lunch break but I was more interested in her story. 'Go on.'

'We'd been intrigued by these swarms of insects. They were

flying in massive clouds and at first we called them flies because they'd settle on anything dead – animal or vegetable – and totally consume it. Like ants or locusts. I've seen them strip one of the cat-sized vertebrates to a clean skeleton, in under an hour. They didn't attack, just settled on what was already dead.'

'Are you saying swarms of insects were the intelligent life?'

She nodded. 'Patty filmed them and analysed their movements. Then she managed to work out a way of communicating with them by using her own body, swaying and stretching and curling up or unfurling her limbs. It was a weird kind of dance, to watch, and you could see the swarm clustering and reshaping in front of her.' She hesitated, and her voice softened. 'A murmuration. Patty showed me a video of these birds we used to have on Earth, starlings. Flying in a huge flock, hundreds of thousands together, wheeling and swooping, so close together it seemed impossible they didn't collide. It took my breath away. She told me no one knew why they did it – they died out in our parents' time. She called these insects a murmuration, after the starlings.'

'So, intelligent like a hive of bees is intelligent.'

She shook her head. 'They farm that planet.'

'How?'

'They maintain a balance between their own numbers and the numbers of the vertebrates whose cadavers they like to feast upon. They eliminate any species which starts to grow too large or develop carnivorous tendencies. They consume fruit and dying vegetation as well. They don't farm so much as – what's the word? – *husband* the planet. Curate it. The detailed knowledge they shared with us was... well, for example, the poisonous fish. There's one kind of fish, I call it a fish but it's more like an eel, which they warned us about, which fulfils a function similar to theirs but underwater. A Cleaner fish which is exceedingly toxic to warm-blooded animals. We hadn't tried to eat any but we had been systematically testing all the aquatic species we came across, and our tests suggested it was harmless.'

'And you believed a swarm of flies rather than scientific tests? I mean, they obviously know how to survive in their environment, but what about problem-solving?'

'Well they fixed our fuel delivery system. They were fascinated by the ship, they swarmed in and crawled all over it, then danced together outside for nearly an hour. Patty said they were communicating with one another – that's thinking, to you and me. When they were ready, they tried to give her instructions, which, being a linguist and not an engineer she couldn't make head nor tail of. So she asked me to give permission for them to fix it themselves.'

I guessed Helena was suffering from dementia. She has scored highly on the brain function and memory tests, but she is already 80 biological years old, and over 120 actual years. We're still not on top of all the physiological and psychological side-effects of prolonged hibernation, and I've come across a couple of other deep space cases where the subject has lost the ability to distinguish between fact and fantasy. I asked her if we could do further screening later in the afternoon.

She grinned. 'It's quite useful for me to have you as a guinea-pig; I thought I might have trouble convincing people. Clearly the idea of a swarm of insects repairing a Mark 6 interstellar light ship stretches your credulity.'

'Just a little.'

'Here's the film.'

She fumbled for her mobile, a full-sized antique model entirely separate from her body. I held it so she could see.

'It's a touch screen – if you tap that arrow the film will play.'

I tapped. The interior of the space ship was well-lit and I could see a dark mass of flying insects descending upon the control panel, obscuring it completely for a moment then lifting off the cover. They flew out of shot and the camera moved into close-up to reveal a single file crawling into a tube which seemed to contain wires. I could see the creatures clearly now, and I should say they were more like bees than flies, with chunky little bodies which they flattened and elongated in order to enter the tube.

'That's the wiring underneath the fuel injector button,' Helena told me. The insects disappeared, one after another, into the tube and more descended from the flying column above, to join them. I could not see any way in which it could have been faked. The reflection of Helena, filming on her mobile, was visible in the blank

25

screen above the control panel.

'I believe you,' I said. The insects stopped entering the tube, presumably because there were enough of them in there to do whatever they were going to do. Helena nodded.

'Nothing happens for the next five minutes – can you fast forward?'

'Just tell me.'

'They started to crawl out again, one by one, exactly as they went in. The swarm did a complicated dance for Patty and she told Chris to start up the inflight systems in a particular order – I think it was ventilation first then fuel – and everything worked. They'd fixed it. None of us understood how.'

'They were intelligent.'

'Yes. Intelligent enough to maintain their own planet as a perfect eco-system. We broke open a flask of wine that evening, to celebrate, and while Patty was trying to explain alcohol to the swarm they flew right around her and completely engulfed her. They were only centimetres from her face but I could see she was laughing. Afterwards she told me it was the most wonderful moment of her life, being enfolded by the swarm. 'Like being hugged by someone who really loves you,' she said.'

I'm not wrong, am I? Last night I dreamed about Edena, the fourth planet in the Delta Pavonis system. I dreamed a wilderness, choked with vines and creepers and rotting fruit, stalked by vicious misshapen carnivores. Insect free.

# Ouroboros

## Ian R. MacLeod

Like most computer geeks, I started out as a hacker. If you're old enough, you may even remember some of my teenage efforts. I specialised in inserting the titles of imaginary new works into the digital catalogues of the world's great museums and libraries. It was all rather neat. I'd create emulations of the system's curator-bots, and send them rattling off along the lattices of virtual shelves. There was *More Ado About Something*, and *Lear's Revenge*, not to mention the fifth movement of Beethoven's Ninth Symphony, *Ode to Agony*, and Tolstoy's little-known sequel, *War and/or Peace*. Great fun, and those early "successes" even allowed me to set up a security consultancy, and launch myself into what briefly seemed like a promising career.

I soon discovered, however, that being a gatekeeper is much harder work, and far less exciting, than messing around with other people's data, and also something for which – in a deeply competitive field – I didn't even possess any particular flair. Of course, I toyed with the idea of doing some proper, serious, criminally-motivated hacking, but I knew in my heart that I lacked the ruthless courage. So instead I spent an alarming number of years working through a variety of commissions in the field which was then still optimistically known Artificial Consciousness, and made my own small contribution toward what is now universally regarded as a dead end. No matter how vast and clever the machine, it turns out that it's impossible to replicate whatever that odd glimmer is we all have going on inside our heads.

Still, I kept a real, proper office right in the heart of Old London, in part because I'd once liked to think of myself as a sort of cybernetic gun-for-hire (*The Maltese Flagon* being another of my favourite fictional fictions), and sat up above the flooded streets on the twentieth floor, vaguely hoping that some mysterious, glamorous visitor would turn up unannounced. What I got instead was an ancient monk.

His head was shaved and he wore dusty crimson robes which were wet at the edges, and his back was hunched and his hands trembled and he was breathing heavily from the long climb up the windy stairs, but nevertheless he possessed the sort of timeless composure you might expect of such a person, and favoured me with a crumpled paper smile that probably wasn't a smile at all as he eased himself down into the chair opposite my desk. Instead of a mala bracelet, tikala mark, cross or Star of David, he wore a carved jade representation of a dragon, which I was later to discover was called Ouroboros, consuming its own tail on a string around his neck.

If I'm honest, my immediate thought was of some grave act of blasphemy I'd committed back when I was a hacking kid. Not that I'd ever gone particularly far in that direction, but I did have *Torah, Torah, Torah* and *Quran: The Corrected Edition* on my CV. Of course, the business model he represented was well on its back foot. I mean, who needs old-fashioned religion when you can enter the gates of Heaven, feast in Valhalla, unite the deserts tribes into the One Truth Faith, or even endure the punishments of Hell – if that's your kind of thing – all for the price of a VR suit? Still, and for no other reason than his quietly assured manner, and my current lack of other clients, I decided to treat this wizened creature with a little respect.

"You're an expert in data and computing," he announced without preamble in a rustling voice, and it was hard to tell whether this was a question or a statement, or something else entirely, his browned face was so wrinkled and hard to read.

"That's what I like to think."

"There were those false creations you once attributed to some of the world's great artists. Michelangelo, Hemmingway and so forth."

"Yes. That was me."

"Indeed. But did you ever consider actually trying to create some of the works to go with those intriguing titles?"

"Well..." In truth, the whole project had begun with that silly dream. But even a few sparse lines or brushstrokes – the grossest, simplest parody – had turned out to be beyond me. So the titles had just got sillier instead. *The Sistine Restrooms* and *Deeper Throat* being later examples of my oeuvre. "No"

"I'm well aware of your work in both its strengths and limitations," the monk said, looking at me in much the same way that one of his kind might regard an ant before they flicked it gently away. "Which is why I have a commission for which I believe you are particularly suited."

Then he just sat there, and I realised he was expecting me to respond. But I certainly wasn't going to fall into the trap of agreeing to something before I knew what it was. In any case, I reckoned I was finally ahead of him.

"Let me guess," I said, "you want me to help you create – or re-create, or invent, however you choose to put it – the mind of God?"

He did smile slightly at that. "I suppose that might once have been an interesting theoretical proposition. But hasn't a great deal of your work in recent years been devoted to proving that such a thing isn't possible? I mean, if machines can't even model the consciousness of a fruit fly, let alone a being as complex as us, what chance would they possibly have with creating God?"

Once again, I was that ant. Not that the virtualities didn't offer their subscribers the chance to have a go at being Jehovah once they'd put up with being Jesus, but that was hardly the same thing.

"Also," he continued, "the core scriptures all tell us that we ourselves, and not some soulless computer, were created in the image of God."

I nodded as if I was still following him, although of course I wasn't. Instead, my mind was slipping in the direction of some virtual Garden of Eden, or perhaps the torture chambers of Torquemada, even though such things had been done to death.

"What I would like you to do is really quite simple," the monk said. "At heart, you're still a hacker, and this is biggest imaginable hack. I would like you to try to break into our universe. And when I say *universe*, I mean everything which you and I and everyone else in this world are currently experiencing…" He gestured tremblingly around my office, then beyond its windows toward the gleaming, flooded city with its rotting towers. "I do hope that's clear?"

I had nothing better to do, and my monk assured me he'd return in exactly a month. But I'm not stupid, and I already knew this whole reality-is-just-a-simulation thing had been around for centuries, and was a popular conceit in many old novels and movies. But I was surprised to discover that it also had some intellectual credence. After all, and even though we humans might not see it that way, our universe is essentially a quantum froth down at its most basic level, formed from an irreducible pixel-like grid. Then there's the way so many things about it still refuse to make proper sense. Gravity not fitting in with the other fundamental forces, for example, or all that missing dark energy and matter. The more I looked into this, the more I was reminded of the sort of fudges and workarounds you'll find in even the most elegantly designed virtual reality.

Soon, I was beginning to understand how fascinating it would be to hack through here-and-now's thin veil. You could shake hands with God, or at least peer into the fuggy bedroom of the alien geek who's running us on his laptop on some rainy Sunday afternoon. But there were more practical possibilities. Imagine what you could do if you possessed the cheat codes to reality. Faster that light travel, unlimited energy? Not a problem. Immortality, likewise. Still, I couldn't help thinking that what my monk really needed was one of those big old-fashioned atom-smashing cyclotrons if he wanted to poke a hole through to next door. But then surely such devices would have succeeded already, if it could be done? I grew discouraged, and probably would have given up entirely if it hadn't been for the evident faith which my monk had placed in me.

After all, I just dealt with computers, data… But hadn't Galileo himself (non-author of *My Travels With A Telescope*) said that God was a mathematician, and wasn't data all everything really amounted to? Rather like my monk's tail-consuming dragon, I was almost back to where I'd started, but my old hacker instincts had returned.

This, I realised, was just a fancier version of hacking the Library of Congress. All I needed was a system which could briefly emulate a sector of reality with sufficient precision and speed to cause its buffers to overrun. You'd get an exploitative weakness, a way right through. I was optimistic. I was excited. Or at least, I was until I tried modelling the idea through some of my computers, and they spat it out with contempt. Turns out that by trying to run a quicker, faster system – my hacking program – inside the system it's in – the universe – I was bumping up against some very fundamental mathematical rules. Ever heard of the *Entscheidungsproblem*? Me neither. But the answer is one big, fat no. And then my month was up. And my monk returned.

Somehow, though, I still wasn't greatly surprised when he simply settled his trembling hands within his robes, and smiled at me.

Now, I awake before dawn to humming chants and rattle of prayer wheels in a place of high, white mountains and deep blue chasms. We novitiates, male and female, are drawn from all the worldly disciplines. Of course, there are mathematicians, priests, poets, virtual engineers and experts in geometries both real and unreal. But there are also farmers, doctors, labourers and beggars – even a few ex-hackers such as myself. Many of us did not even realise before we came here that we had lost all hope.

First we must deal with the usual morning matters of order, cleanliness and food, which are followed by a period of preparatory prayer. There is, of course, still a machine at the heart of our endeavour, an intricate, constantly-expanding device, capable and vast, which reaches far beyond this monastery – out into space and the furthest corners of the world. It rides the vast, ever-growing seas of information. It enters the slow minds of the devices which crawl the depths of the oceans, and dances with the nanobots which ride the highest currents of the air. And we novitiates are the ghosts in that machine. We are the grit which will form the pearl.

Deep inside the mountain beneath our monastery there is a cave, and within that cave there is a small jade pyramid, and within that pyramid there is an ebony box, and within that box there is a minute gold sphere, and within that sphere there is nothing, or as close to nothing as can be physically created in ordinary space. This is the core of the mandala, this is the still point upon which the power of all our minds, along with a vast suite of sensors, modelling and monitoring devices, are focussed. Hacking is a crude and unnecessary term. For here lies the Bindu, the centre of everything, and we have already detected slight but nevertheless measurable perturbations within its quantum froth.

None of us know, as we finally arise from meditation and bells ring out amid the golds and indigos of sunset, just how long this task will take. But I am already sure, as I stoop to wash my face in a porcelain bowl, and the beginnings of a wizened countenance I'm starting to recognise gazes back at me, that we will, one day, succeed.

*Author's dedication*: thanks to Benedict Durrant for pointing me in the direction of the *Entscheidungsproblem*

# The Escape Hatch

## Matthew De Abaitua

In her video, she called it 'the escape hatch'. It appeared one morning when she was driving to her temporary teaching job at the university. Beside the A12, the dawn mist obscured the legs of the pylons, their latticed towers seemed to be floating across the field. She was probably speeding, she would admit that much, trying to outrun the news on the radio – the Chinese economic collapse, the acid shores of the Indian Ocean, allegiance trials on the banks of the Mississippi. The road dipped toward Chelmsford, and there it was - a semi-circular section of what she described in her video as half a black sun or a protractor of negative space. The traffic ahead disappeared into it. Rachel slowed but did not stop. In her rearview mirror, she saw a truck jackknife across both lanes. In that instant, it seemed more dangerous to stop suddenly than to continue. "It was as if space-time was a jigsaw with a missing piece," she said to her creative writing channel and her thousands of subscribers, her Bartlebabies.

Her Bartlebabies wanted to know where she found the courage to just drive right in. There was no simple answer. Her heart was a diagram of tensions, her mother's controlling personality pulling in one direction, her hourly-paid temporary position in another. The bald tyres on her old Toyota were a point on that diagram, as was Dan's suggestion that they call timeout on their relationship so that he could experiment with Tindr. Maybe, over the last fifty metres, she even tapped the accelerator. The black sun was beautiful. Like a solar eclipse sliding into a slot.

She withdrew her feet from the pedals, gripped the wheel, closed her eyes and drove onward, thinking: *whatever this is, maybe it's better than what I've got.*

Her car emerged on the other side, the tyres kicking up a cloud of golden dust. Ahead, other cars had parked up, doors open, drivers and passengers staggering around open-mouthed under a white sky. She drove slowly onward then parked up on a mesa of golden stone. In the white sky there were two black moons set apart like peep holes for a gargantuan voyeur. She killed the engine and sat there, hardly daring to breathe, in case the oxygen inside the car was all the oxygen she had left. Her heart was an organ of anxiety at the best of times. Seeing that the other people still showed no ill effects other than shock, she wound down the side window and took her first breath on another planet. It felt good. If it was toxic, then this was a toxicity that was also a cure, like a gin and tonic.

She walked over to a man leaning against the bonnet of his German car; the over-exposed sky at his back made his dark suit merge into the black metal of the chassis. He was squinting at his phone, but sensed her approach.

"Do you have any water?" he said, in a low voice. "We might run out of water. If you have water then we should make a deal."

He did not look up. He was talking to his phone as much as he was talking to her. She looked back at the way she had come; the dust clouds drifted away and there was the other side of the escape hatch, the half-disc slid into the golden rock like a giant coin going into the slot of a vending machine. There were no more arrivals. She remembered the lorry jack-knifing in the rear view mirror. The A12 would be an accident scene. The question was... Well, there were a thousand questions obviously... but the most immediate was this: did the escape hatch open only one-way? Because if it did, then it was only a matter of time before this man with the German car nominated himself as the acceptable face of cannibalism.

She returned to her car, did a three-point turn, and drove slowly back. Passing through the escape hatch felt like solitude, an attentive aloneness that came to an end abruptly and left her with a sense of loss. She parked up on the other side of the A12. The road was cordoned off, blue flashing lights around the wreck of the lorry. This was where she recorded her video, holding her phone at arm's length, set to selfie, the black sun at her back, other people walking through it.

"There's another planet and we can walk there," she said, her voice angry with wonder. "The planet is habitable and I've seen it.

We don't need a spaceship or a government. This will be our amazing world and we can reach it through this –" she gestured at the semi-circle of negative space, saw how nameless it was "– this *escape hatch.*" She turned around and zoomed in on the golden dust clouds drifting through the black space, their particles glittering violently.

Within the hour, Rachel's video had clocked up a hundred million views.

People came from all over to see the escape hatch. The initial police blockade was not enough to stop people as they hiked across the fields and lanes. When the army sealed off the area, people hired planes to fly through it, and when the airspace was patrolled by the Royal Airforce, some even went along old tunnels underground and discovered the lower semi-circle of the escape hatch down there. Why, she asked her Bartlebabies, was the first concern of the government to stop people going through? Just because the escape hatch had appeared on British territory, did it really fall under the jurisdiction of a national government? What right did they have to do this? If the escape hatch constituted first contact or an act of communication, then what message was the government sending by sealing it off from its own citizens in this way?

Inspired by her video, more people pressed against the barricades until they broke through. The army and the police didn't know what to do. They understood how to protect property and the sanctity of the state. The escape hatch was neither of those things. The Prime Minister arrived by helicopter; against the advice of her press team, she stepped through the escape hatch and spent an hour on the other planet. When she came out, she sighed, as if disappointed to be back. The people saw it in her eyes, she wanted to escape too.

In the streets and the shops, strangers recognised Rachel and looked at her hungrily: *what was it like,* they asked, but in their eyes there was a more urgent question: *is it better than this?*

Her videos racked up millions of views. By the end of the month she would be rich. The university wanted to speak to her about a permanent position. Dan called her, and confessed that he had hated every minute of the time-out and that he wanted to see her right away. Maybe they could experiment with Tindr together? She wasn't sure about Dan but she was famous now, and her videos were attracting as much bad attention as good. Dan was a creep but - as her mother always said - better the creep you know.

Dan came over and she listened to his self-justification about the time-out, how being apart from her had really opened his eyes. But when he said this, she saw that his eyes were glinting with same question as all the others: *is it better than this?*

"We should return to the escape hatch together," said Dan, brushing his hand against her arm, testing if he could retake possession of her. "We can film it as we cross over to the other side," Dan put his arms around her. "You can lead us."

"Why?"

"Because you discovered the hatch. You're like Neil Armstrong or Christopher Columbus."

"Christopher Columbus did not discover anything."

"Neil Armstrong didn't discover the moon either but everyone knows that it's his footprint right *there*. You said it yourself, they've already taken the Earth from us, why should they get this planet too?"

If their relationship was a diagram then his need to control her was one point, and her acceptance of control was another, and the fact that she found all this control exhausting was the crucial third point that introduced tension. But he wasn't wrong. She had as much right to visit this planet as anyone. There were so many names for the new planet but no consensus. Because whoever named it would control it. This was a real world and it belonged to nobody, and so it shouldn't have a name, not yet; she wanted the unnamed planet, heart and soul. The longing was thrilling and terrifying, her smile was determined and so was the glint in Dan's eye. They would return to the escape hatch.

First, she had to calm down. She went into the bathroom, filled the sink and immersed her face in her cold reflection, held her breath and listened to the beat of her anxiety. It was regular, that was something. She came up for air, towelled off her face, and it was then that she noticed, lowdown in her reflection in the bathroom mirror, the semi-circular gap.

At first, she thought a piece had fallen out of the mirror. But when she touched it, she realised the mirror was intact. This semi-circular section of negative space was in her collarbone. She pulled her hair back urgently so that she could take a closer look. She stepped away from the mirror and looked down but the small black half-sun was too high on her collarbone for her to see it with her own eyes, no matter how much she twisted around. She would have to touch it. Slowly, she lowered her fingertips into the space. It felt warmer in there. There was no pain. She reached in deeper - if the hole had been cored into her body then her fingers would have reached her lungs. But all she could touch was alien air. When she withdrew her hand, it was sheathed in golden dust.

At a press conference on the A12, a journalist asked the Prime Minister if the escape hatch was safe. "The people expect the government to be in control of any eventuality," she said. "It's time the people grew up." When she smiled, her mouth was an inverted protractor of negative space. The government lifted the barricade to let the people come and go through the escape hatch at will. The first truckloads of colonists arrived, emblazoned with homemade art and flanked by daytrippers bearings flags and streamers. No life had been discovered on the planet. The atmospheric probe that had penetrated the white sky was lost. Its last readings suggested that a habitable area totalling almost two hundred and fifty thousand square kilometres existed around the escape hatch. The edge of this territory was a vertical black sea. The first man to swim in this black sea was later washed up on Dover beach: bemused, exhausted but alive.

In the bathroom, Rachel buttoned her shirt all the way up to her collar. If the appearance of this negative space in her body was a side effect of her travelling through the escape hatch, then she would tell no one, not even Dan could know. She would ask him to leave before he discovered it.

A part of her remained behind on the planet and she was entangled with it, like two points in a diagram. After each visit, another part of her would remain on the golden planet. The exchange made sense. Its logic reassured her. She packed her rucksack and filled up three water bottles. She told Dan she would meet him at the railway station. But she didn't. She walked along the A12, through the stalled traffic and crowds and food stalls, and the faces of the people around her were concentrated upon a single note of longing.

# Childhood's Friend

## Rachel Pollack

At first they were just knobs. Once the babies got hair, the doctors said, no one would even see them. Apparently, our parents were very concerned about this. "We just want them to have normal lives," they said. We know this because at one point we sent ourselves (not our bodies, of course) back to observe those meet-ups with pre-parents and doctors. 'Just normal' became a kind of slogan that we broadcast across the system. We only did this for fun, but we must have accidentally used the *human* system, because a bunch of Important People assembled a bunch of *us* – I think we were four or five years old – to ask us "please" could we not "mess up" their grid? That was how they thought children talked.

I remember how much their anger and confusion – and fear they'd made a terrible mistake – tickled the sides of my knobs. Well, all our knobs, of course, but we had just begun to focus and we each still thought of our experiences as singular in some way.

"Enhancements," the doctors said in those early conversations with our parents. Apparently, enhancement was a big idea at the time. Humans enhanced – made bigger – parts of their bodies they thought other humans would find appealing. But this was different, the doctors said. These enhancements would give us *abilities*. Maths, science, music, language – there were always humans who could do special things. Compose complicated music almost impossible to perform, except for others who could play it, all by the age of 5, and without ever taking lessons. Some solved equations and other puzzles. One man recited the digits of $\pi$ up to fifty thousand numbers, without hesitation, over two weeks. Others could name the day of the week for any given date, no matter how far in the past or the future.

And then there were people who were *many* people – like us, we thought excitedly, except they were all jammed into one body, so more like the opposite of us – some of which knew things, like other languages, that none of the others, especially the 'originals', had ever learned. Others could fix any machine, no matter how broken or complicated, even if they'd never seen it before. "These kinds of abilities," the doctors would say, in a fever of excitement, "they're almost like super-powers!"

That was the point at which the parents always got upset (oh, how they cherished the idea that every one of them was unique – but then, we used to think so, too). They would say things like, "These people – aren't they, you know, damaged?"

"Yes, yes, of course," the doctors said. "No one wants to damage your baby. We're *doctors*." What they'd done, they said, was study the chemicals and nervous systems of such people to *isolate* (the doctor pointed a finger at my future mother as he said this, I don't know why) the sources of these powers, and then separate them from 'ordinary function and personality'. The knobs, they said, would contain the 'potentialities' and allow the child to 'draw' on them without suffering any 'trauma'.

And they were such *little* knobs, the doctors promised – hardly more than modules.

For some reason, I think of the girl who was found drawing diagrams on her knobs with crayons one day. Her mother took away the crayons and scrubbed the knobs, but not before Daddy photographed what she'd drawn. A couple of weeks later the telescope people released the same image. "The oldest ever discovered," they said. The girl – Ursula, I think they called her – was three.

Some (potential) parents refused. Once, a bunch of us tried to go back and witness the doctors giving their thrilling super-power speech to parents who turned us down. The best we could do was observe parents who said "No" at first, but then gave in later. It was sad to think there could have been more of us. And then it was funny! Because after all, every one of us is all of us.

We didn't know that at first. Not for years, actually, not even when we discovered each other. We each had a Mommy and a Daddy who tried to 'stimulate' us following some plan by the teams of 'Darwin's Helpers', as the researchers liked to call themselves.

They were "advancing humanity," they said, "harvesting disabilities and transforming them into potentialities." They had a softball team, and that's what they called it, 'Darwin's Helpers'. Every few weeks they would test us, and then give the parents a new set of instructions.

Some of the parents, the fathers mostly, asked about physical enhancements. They wanted to 'harvest' someone named Le Bron James. Darwin's Helpers told them it wasn't about individual talents. Actually, I think they tried, but this Bron person (and the others they asked) told them to go away. Or their lawyers did.

There was lots of discussion about whether we should go to school. Be with other children. Mingle. It would have to be a special 'gifted' school, of course. Most of us could read and write in several languages, some unknown, by the age of two, and when we got together – something the parents didn't really like – we sometimes did the π thing as a kind of game, picking up where we'd left off the last time, and chanting the numbers faster and faster until we laughed so much we had to stop.

I think Darwin's Helpers wanted us to go to some special camp, maybe with walls and super-security (as if that could stop us). But the parents vetoed that. They'd all signed a contract which gave them that right, and then they'd formed some club or something to make joint decisions. "Normal lives," they insisted. "Live in the world." Oh, if they only *knew!* They had no idea what the 'world' actually was.

So there we went, off to school, with bright super-hero lunch boxes, and new clothes, and instructions to make sure we kept our hair combed over the knobs. Though no one said it, part of the idea was not just for us to 'mingle', with 'other' children (the word 'normal' was forbidden), but to keep us away from each other. Our bond was not 'healthy', that was one thing the parents and Darwin's Helpers all agreed upon. So we let them think that not being in the same place kept us apart. But you know how they harvested the 'skills' of lots of people all sharing one body? Well, we could do that, it was fun, but we also could be one person sharing lots of bodies.

The hair trick didn't work very well. Most of us got noticed right away. Maybe that wouldn't have happened, at least so soon, if

41

the plan to keep us secret hadn't fallen apart just after we started school. It seems that one of Darwin's Helpers discovered he had one of the speedier kinds of cancer, and he wanted to get credit before he died. So he held a press conference, and he even invited a few of us (without telling our parents – lawsuits! – but he was dying anyway) to come and do tricks – recite Bible passages in a bunch of languages, solve fancy equations, play music only we could understand – stuff like that.

As well as lawsuits, there were committees, and hearings, and people shouting and waving signs. But really, the important thing was that people knew about the knobs. All our parents' plans to hide them, and to act 'normal', fell apart. "Knobblies," they called us. Then they would knock us down and call us "Knobbly-Wobblies." Some teachers yelled, some pretended not to notice. Some resigned.

One of us got set on fire. Charcoal lighter fluid poured over the horns, followed by matches. She called out to us and we changed the air so the fire would die out before it could hurt her, but I guess some of the normal kids found it hard to breathe for a bit – well, it all led to more hearings, more marches, more laws, more soldiers...and most of us leaving school.

We didn't mind. It was right after this that we saw the Cloud. Maybe the trick with the air was what did it, but once we noticed it we realized it was all around us, everywhere, and yet somehow just out of reach. That was frustrating, but I remember how exciting it was when we realized *all* of us could see it.

And hear it. A whisper, up in the sky, in the walls, underneath our parents' voices, inside machines, even in our own blood. The whispers were telling us something but we couldn't understand it. Those of us who were lots of selves began to cycle through them (and make some new ones) to try and find one that could hear better, or maybe recognize a language. None of the human selves worked, so we tried trees, thinking maybe the branches could reach inside the cloud. (I was a tree for several days once, when I was four – I stopped because my parents thought I'd died.) When that didn't work we went back to animals. Maybe doggie smell, or cat hearing, would do it. Only snakes seemed to get any closer, as if the cloud was on the ground and not in the sky. Some of us thought we should stay serpenty, but after a while we had to realize that wasn't going to do it.

And then we tried insects. We lay down in the dirt, our bodies kind of hardened, and the knobs – the knobs focused, and twitched, and reached out – and found the message. "Sharpen."

Of course! The knobs were too blunt. Silly, silly. We focused on them, growing neurons, opening pathways, and stretching the skin, and even the bone, to contain it all. And that's how the knobs became horns. Not curly, like a cow or a ram, or branchy, like a deer, but sharp cones that sparkled with golden light. Our skin colour stayed, but now it sparkled – black with gold shining through – brown with gold – beige or pink – but always light, sharper than the Sun. At least for us. As it turned out, most of the humans just saw the horns. They didn't like that. They had some kind of history with horns.

But we didn't care. Or even notice at first. For us, we'd discovered that the light was the cloud, and it filled our bodies even as our horns penetrated it. The cloud wasn't a thing, it was a network.

There was so much going on! Marches, fires, but we didn't care about that. We were still trying to understand it all. We still needed to know what the cloud *wanted*.

Then the government helped. And our parents. The government rounded us up and our parents cried, or shouted, or wailed and hugged us, and finally said it was all for the best (Oh, it was, it was!). A few tried to hold out, took their kids, and some rifles, and boxes of food and bullets, and headed for the woods (or the desert, or caves, or even sewers), but none of them lasted very long. They would hug us, and cry like all the others, and say "Maybe it really is all for the best..." Their kids held their breaths and didn't say anything except things like "It's okay, Daddy. I love you," trying not to show how excited they were. Because of course the whole time they were hiding in their daddies' secret places, they could hear *us* in their heads, saying "Come on! We're all waiting for you. Hurry up!"

At last we were all together. There were cabins, and doctors, and a big metal fence, and guards with guns. To protect us, they

43

said. Of course, we could leave any time we wanted to. But we were together! Now the cloud changed, separated, took on forms. Children. They were us! "Finally," they said. "Now we can begin."

# Takes from the White Hart

## Bruce Sterling

Every lost soul aboard the "Brexitania" had plenty of cause for drink. We'd been out to sea, off and on, ever since that terrible referendum. Then I realized that someone wanted to tell me a science fiction story in the ship's bar.

I was once a hard-working journalist – (on the environmental beat, back when smart people still pretended that the Earth would get saved). A journalist always loves indiscreet confessions.

Alert readers might imagine that "Harry Purvis" was motivated to tell me his story for the price of a drink. Why? Because that was the motivating gimmick in the classic "Jorkens" stories of Edward Drax Plunkett, Lord Dunsany. There are a hundred and fifty of those witty, tricky Dunsany stories, which were all written between 1925 and 1957.Even though "Jorkens" himself is clearly a pitiful, penniless alcoholic, those are terrific fantasy stories: even Arthur C. Clarke liked to re-write "Jorkens" stories. Jorkens will never be bettered when it comes to weird, trippy bar yarns.

But Lord Dunsany was a big-game hunter, a chess master, a toff, and an Irish Renaissance dramatist. Dunsany could listen to endless stories from weird drunks in bars, because he had all kinds of aristocratic credibility to back him up. Also, Dunsany's readers had nothing better to do with their twentieth-century time than to peruse some "Jorkens" bar stories.

Our globalized bar aboard the "Brexitania" was highly fantastic, too, but in an urgent, jittery, painfully modern way.

In the year 2017, who could sit down in Dunsany's literate tradition of "Jorkens" and narrate a ripping yarn with a cool twist-ending? Was that feat of Irish oral culture even physically possible for us?

Probably not! Consider a classic science-fiction story, of the standard six thousand word length (the normal size intended for the standard pulp-digest magazine format). Even at a gabby conversational rate of two hundred words a minute, that means that somebody, somehow, is listening to a story told in a bar, with respectful, rapt attention, never once touching their cellphone, for thirty solid minutes! How? Who would ever have the patience for that now?

We were exiles on the "Brexitania," marooned at sea on our storm-tossed, illegal cruise ship. But despite our seasick tedium, we lacked means, motive and opportunity to hearken to any elaborate works of oral fiction. Because we were all thumb-twitchingly busy on social media, watching Britain convulse in political and economic crisis.

We were Russian speculators, German industrialists, Arab princes, Chinese Party exiles, European spouses undergoing painful divorces; I was an unemployed Texan freelance journalist on an overstayed tourist visa who was living off Bitcoin.

We, the sly denizens of our ship-of-fools, had five hundred different fact-free, fake-news reasons for hiding out aboard the "Brexitania." Most of us imagined we'd done something dazzling clever by evading local British regulations. That's because we all believed in our social media filter-bubbles. These cultish political illusions were like science fiction bar-stories, only far bigger and vastly more dangerous.

Being exiles, we were naturally paranoid, so we rarely let our guard down for any face-to-face confrontations. Except for "Harry Purvis," that is – although, obviously, that wasn't his true name. "Purvis" was roommates with a Sinhalese Sri Lankan guy in a dhoti loincloth who somehow called himself "Charles Willis." Nobody ever saw "Purvis" and "Willis" in company together, so we all presumed that "Purvis" and "Willis" were somehow the same guy with two different border-skipping passports.

Our allegedly-British cruise ship was really "Panamanian," obviously. Although we called her the "Brexitania," she had scraped-off, face-lifted pseudonyms on her bow: she'd once been known as the "Valency" and the "Sea Spray." She was older than the Suez Crisis. Those aboard her were a scurvy crew of chancers, demimondaines, remittance men, wide boys and tax bandits.

"Harry Purvis" tried to entertain our lurching shipboard crowd with fantastic bar-stories that he imagined were weirder than our existent, physical situation. That was his habit. As I dawdled with a shot of whiskey, I saw "Purvis" approaching me.

He wanted to tell his unusual story – but this isn't the heyday of Lord Dunsany or Dr. Clarke, this is the present day. I can't buy "Purvis" a drink as an icebreaker, so that he can relate his weird tale, which he's obviously dying to tell me.

On the Brexitania, we're not allowed to buy people any drinks. The many Arab princes aboard, who are mostly Libyan and Moroccan victims of the Arab Spring, can never be seen buying booze, because Sharia. So the Arabs just discreetly run an open tab for everybody; they regard Scotch single-malt as an unending natural resource, something like North Sea Oil.

I'm ready to listen to "Purvis" – because, as a journalist, I'm keen on people rashly blurting terrible things that might ruin them. So I haul out my big analog tape recorder and make a professional-courtesy deal out of turning it on for him, even though, just like everybody, I've got an Android with built-in recording capacity that does real-time voice recognition and transcription, typing up every eavesdropped word neatly and posting it into my encrypted Dropbox.

With a little journalistic thumb-work I can upload my secret snapshots of "Harry Purvis," and the chances are quite high that Google Images or Facebook will recognize his face and tell me who "Purvis" really is. "Purvis" has that haunted look of an offshored celebrity under a thin incognito.

The deal with a fantastic bar story, though – (I mean, the basic payoff for the subgenre) – is that "Purvis" must tell me his bar story, and, naturally, I can't believe what he says. However, I'm unable to figure out the careful shadings between the plausible and the incredible. It's this trompe l'oeil aesthetic effort that's the game between author and reader.

Because – (bear with me here, this digression is important) – what if the seemingly normal parts of the story are pure convention, they're made up? While the story's "fantastic" element is a genuine, quotidian thing that happens every day? Even though it's the part you can't possibly believe, the "fantasy" is stone-obvious, it's genuine social truth.

Consider this: the Atlantic weather outside our cruise ship is obviously terrible and getting worse fast, but we never tell each other that our fake-glamorous lifestyle is doomed by climate change. There's way too much objectively verifiable science in that idea. We can't handle the reality.

Clearly it's something much along these lines that "Harry Purvis" must relate to me. He's planning a genuinely edgy, truly subversive revelation.

The harsh truth is: "Harry Purvis" is not even drunk. The whole business of setting a sci-fi story inside a pub is a mere, faked-up, literary convention.

Granted, science fiction authors, like most too-smart depressives, tend to drink too much. So it's "plausible," sure. However, that literate mannerism with the British "pub," and the conviviality, and the people buying each other rounds of tepidly warm Newcastle Brown Ale, or whatever – it's all there as a diegetic mechanism. The story's drunken atmosphere is just an invocation, to trick the reader into a mentally reckless mood of suspended disbelief.

It's not just science fiction writers who pull this stunt. Consider those endless Manhattan cocktail-swilling scenes in the American TV series "Sex and the City," where the four overdressed New York women need to confess unbelievable things about kinked relationships with men. Those four female protagonists are always story-telling in bars.

But check this out: if one of their "Sex in the City" men turns out to be a time traveller, or if he's a zombie, fantastic vampire, or kind-hearted billionaire bondage sadist who's maybe also a dashing astronaut, well, that fantasy element works out great. That's true even though "Sex and the City" was originally a nonfiction newspaper column by New York journalist Candace Bushnell. Modern fantasy-romance has got ten thousand times the market potential of Lord Dunsany.

But if you watch "Sex and the City" – (which I love to do, because I've been talking all this time as if I was some tough, ironic

Texan journalist, and that's all true, but I'm also a woman, so there) – well, those TV shows date from 1998 to 2004. So, from our own stark 2017 perspective, the weird, unbelievable part is that all these smart NYC gal-pals never haul out a cellphone to check their Instagram feeds. They never shoot a selfie despite their awesome TV-actress make-up. They're downright archaic women.

"Harry Purvis" is not trying to hit on me in the bar, despite my surprise revelation about being a woman. "Harry" wants a narrative first-line hook to start his story with, but our modern ship-of-fools is pitching uncontrollably. Every time the restless ocean gives us one of those sea-sickly surges, "Purvis" skids across our vinyl bar-couch and oozes closer to me. It's a mysterious, unsought, mechanical intimacy. It's like an Amazon recommendation, almost. It's like you've been clicking on a bunch of Arthur Clarke Award prizewinners and Amazon starts recommending obscure British writers who are genuinely terrific, like Barrington Bayley and Anna Kavan.

That's how close "Harry Purvis" and I are getting now. We both know he doesn't have enough word-count left to tell me any cracking sci-fi bar story. Short-short SF stories do exist – of course they do – but they are mostly in-jokes, jingles, gags. They're like a dust-cover blurb; a literary task that authors will spend a hell of a lot of time on, but only for stark careerist reasons.

"Harry Purvis" and I are stuck in a literary purgatory. He's sweating and fretting about that; he's pulling his old-school regimental tie loose; he doesn't know what to do with his hands.

"Purvis" is so visibly anxious that I wonder if, instead of a great science fiction bar story, he's going to offer me some lousy pick-up-artist bar story. Pick-up stories are even faker than science fiction, because they're lies invented by aggressive men to impress the tipsy, emotionally vulnerable women who frequent bars. But no: "Harry Purvis" just can't do that. I'm probably attractive enough to be attacked, exploited and degraded, but this can't become a shipboard seduction story, because me – nameless, dainty little me – well, I'm this story's secondary narrator. I'm supposed to be relating the story of "Purvis" to you in my first-person voice, so I can't possibly become the romantic lead at the same time.

It's all so modern, so confusing: yet it's worse. I'm in one of those woman's-intuition situations where you just know, gut-level, by heart, that the guy before you is in unredeemable trouble. "Purvis" direly needs to sidle over and confide to my willing feminine ear. But our conventional literary structure just won't support that. It's become unspeakable. It's beyond words.

Maybe he's a UFO abductee. Something along that line. Ecstatic. Dreadful. Uncontainable by any British literary tradition. And the American dialect of the English language? The American vernacular is not even in the goddamn ball-park! A completely wrong set of sports metaphors, three strikes you're out! The American language can't even spell "tyre" properly, so it will never convey the burdens of "Harry Purvis."

Suddenly I beckon at "Purvis", mutely. Because I'm a Texan chick, we're bold, we're tough. We Texans have handguns, a huge prison system, we have ghettos, barrios, hurricanes, tornadoes, we have weird military suicide Alamo revenge cults. What is the worst thing that any British fantasist could possibly say to me?

I have just a few precious moments, in my Texan girl-reporter fashion, to second-guess "Harry Purvis."

Are triffids going to blind us and eat us?

Is there an unearthly sentinel, standing with terrible cosmic patience, over a black slab buried in the Moon?

Or is this some weird "inner space" issue? Are car-crash cultists going to surrealistically evert and expose our sexual pop-art hang-ups? Or is this brief bar-story something far beyond all humanity? Is it some great, mountainous, cosmic, Stapledonian vista where post-humans have telepathy and branching fractal fingers and are nevertheless still British?

I reckon that I must be overthinking it, yet then…

# Your Death, Your Way, 100% Satisfaction Guaranteed!

## Emma Newman

When the angel came at the moment of his death, he was pleased to see that her divine beauty was worth every penny he had spent on it. No off-the-shelf avatar for Lucius St John Hampton-York! Not for the most important moments of his life.

He appreciated the irony that these moments were being crammed into the last seconds before the life support machine completed his carefully managed brain death. He didn't want his last thought to be '*if only I'd paid for the top package*'. He'd made that mistake before – but only once. He'd made many over the years, inevitable for anyone who'd amassed a fortune as large as his, but each had only been made once. He was a fast learner, right to the end.

The angel's smile felt like the first sunlight of spring after a bleak winter and he couldn't stop himself smiling back. Her chestnut hair had a hint of auburn, her eyes an iridescent green that could never be found in birth genetics, her skin a pleasing shade of light brown. His critical eye considered how the most appealing features represented a memorial to his failed marriages. It jarred him, to think that the software running this 'immersive' had rifled through his neocortex, plucking out physical features that obviously still triggered something in his hind brain. It reminded him of his grandmother rifling through tins of ancient family photographs, one of the last generation with a life expectancy below 100.

He had celebrated his 140th last month, from his hospice bed, a raucous affair involving a water slide filled with champagne that emptied into a pool surrounded by old fashioned burlesque stars applauding his every exit from the tube. That was his own private virtual party, the one the family didn't know about, enjoyed after the tedious virtual dinner he'd had with them. How a steak that didn't even exist could cost as much as one in the real goddamn restaurant fifty years ago had made him rant. And all of his family had been forced to sit there and listen and agree with him. Even now, it still made him smile.

"Lucius, it's time, darling," the angel said with the voice of his mother. Tears sprang into his eyes for the first time in over a hundred years.

"Momma," he croaked, forgetting the software.

"Yes, darling, I've come to take you with me." Even as she spoke, the eyes had turned blue, her hair was getting blonder by the moment, and then he was sobbing in her arms like a little boy again. That embrace, that feeling of being enveloped in love and safety and comfort, was one he'd craved so many times since she'd died. Now he didn't care about the pillaging of old memories, he was glad of it. The angel even smelt of her floral soap as her wings wrapped around him, cocooning him.

"It's time to say goodbye," she said softly.

"No, Momma, not again," he sobbed but she laughed and said "Not to me, darling, I'm not leaving you again."

He felt stupid, dragging his hands across his cheeks to wipe away tears his brain thought was there but were not. The embarrassment snapped him back into himself, made him imagine some intern in a data centre monitoring the exchange. That's what the top package really meant, wasn't it? That this angel's words were being monitored in real time, rather than being left to whatever the AI came up with. Or maybe there was someone roleplaying as his mother, watching his brain activity light up in all the places it should, laughing as-

"Lucius, you can't put it off any longer. Don't think too hard about it all. Death is acceptance, a letting go, remember?"

"All right, I'll see them."

Somehow a sofa appeared, a cloud-soft place for him to sit with the angel's maternal arms still around him. She seated herself behind him, allowing him to lean back in her embrace, as he used to lean against his momma to watch musicians play in her rehearsal space. Then a room phased into existence around them and he realised they weren't actually in a place before. It was like her old studio, only filled with his favourite pieces of furniture collected over the years. The window looked out over the sea instead of a grimy brick wall, everything so clean, so perfect. He sighed with pleasure.

When he looked away from the window, his daughter stood in front of them. On his favourite rug. He opened his mouth to tell her to move before remembering it wasn't the real rug. That was lost in a fire over seventy years ago. He could still remember how his first wife left him over it. How he'd lain down on it, stroking the silk pile as she hurled abuse from the bedroom while packing her case. How he'd felt certain he'd picked the right design as the front door slammed shut behind her. How perfect that sense of satisfaction was.

"Daddy," Collette said, managing a smile. She wore a nice suit his assistant picked out for her, brimming with a fifty year old's youth he could only dimly recall. "I wanted to say thank you for everything you've done for me. I know you haven't been happy with some of the decisions I've made over my life, but..."

There was no point reminding her of her flaws. She couldn't hear him, after all.

"But you've... forgiven me and supported me and the children through some really rough patches. And I'll always be grateful for that."

That she doesn't take after her mother still disappointed him. He'd assumed that his third, most beautiful wife would give him the most beautiful kids. That was another mistake he only made once; not checking how much cosmetic surgery she'd had before they married. He'd been so infatuated; he'd thought that those high cheekbones and full lips were written into the genetics she'd mix with his. He couldn't help but shake his head at himself. Well, he wasn't even 80 when he'd made that mistake.

"I'm sorry I can't be with you in person when... when it..." she flicked a strand of red hair from her face, a gesture she did inherit from her mother, alas. "I'm just swamped with the negotiations. Don't worry, I won't forget your values, okay? I'm your girl, remember?"

He smiled at her then, remembering all the times he'd said that to her in person, usually with a hand on her shoulder, just before critical meetings where he'd wanted a softer face of his corporation at the negotiating table.

"Tilly and Rafe are at your bedside, right now. We all love you, Daddy. Give 'em hell in the afterlife, okay?"

She had the grace to look as if she was trying not to cry. It wasn't genuine, but he appreciated the effort. She faded away and he looked at the rug again. Handmade by artisans in some piss poor place he couldn't remember. What artistry. What skill!

A chair appeared, breaking his view, his third son seated in it. Lucius was appalled by how old he looked. Aging 'gracefully' was so distasteful.

"Hi, Dad," Tobias croaked. "Thought I should pay my respects. I wasn't going to, when I heard what you were planning, but... I suppose it's your choice."

Lucius sniggered to himself. Chip off the old block.

"I thought I might regret not saying some things to you. But now I'm recording this, maybe some things shouldn't be said. So I'm just going to say sorry. Which is not something I make a habit of saying. You know who taught me that? You!" He laughed, and his wheeze merged with Lucius's own creaking chuckle.

"I'm sorry we didn't get along. I think I wanted you to be someone you're not. Like, I dunno, a good father." He laughed again and Lucius broke into a full-throated guffaw. "That was my problem, not yours. Now I'm an old toad too, I can see it. So that's my message for you. Go and enjoy the rest of your digitally managed death. See you on the other side soon. Get some decent whiskey in, okay?"

He faded out and Lucius looked at the rug again. He smiled, remembering the women he undressed on the real one, some of whom he was married to. They all blended into one now, a patchwork of long legs and full hips and –

"Are you ready, Lucius?" the angel asked.

"Aren't there any more messages?"

"No. Your family have sent emails. Would you like to read them before we go?"

Only two? But his descendants are busy, successful people. He made sure of that. Better they be out there, continuing his work, than weeping into a camdrone. And there were a couple of great-grandkids with him in the real world. Not that he could remember which ones they are.

"I don't need to read them. I know I was loved. That I was a great man who did magnificent things. I know I have left the world a better place. I don't need them to tell me that."

"Are you ready?"

A flicker of fear passed before he can fully register it. He had a dim recollection of the sales patter that described full emotional management of death. No pain. No fear. Guaranteed.

He stood and took the angel's hands. The room filled with a light coming from behind him. "Look, Lucius," the angel said, and she pointed past his shoulder. "It's time to go –"

She glitched, twitching horribly for a second before she disappeared and he howled at the wrench in his guts. Covering his wet face with his hands, he started mentally composing a searing complaint to the service provider, when the sense of a room around him disappeared, along with that of his hands and face.

After a moment of darkness he found himself in another room that was clinically clean and did not contain his handmade silk rug.

There was a bed surrounded by complicated equipment and two people seated beside it, hunched forwards. It was silent.

A shrivelled husk of a man lay in the bed and Lucius realised that it was *him*, seen from above.

*This isn't what I paid for!* No one responded to his angry shriek and he didn't even hear it. The mouth of the body impossibly below him was slack.

A high-pitched tone filled the air and various lights flashed on the equipment. The two people – Rafe and Tilly, he realised then – jumped up and embraced one another. Just as he started to revel in their howling grief, they parted and he saw that they were sobbing with happiness, cheering with joy at his passing.

*I did not pay for this!* He shrieked again, hollowly.

Tilly tapped the air, interfacing with her neural chip, and swiped her hand toward the wall where an image was projected of her great grandmother, dressed in the suit she was wearing when she recorded the message for him.

"He's dead!" Tilly cried. "The old bastard is dead!"

The joyful relief on Collette's face was undeniable. "I'll let them know. It starts today, kids. Everything's going to get so much better. I promise!"

He looked at Rafe, hoping to see a hint of grief, but the boy was putting on lipstick. When Tilly looked at him, Collette saw him too.

And she smiled. She *smiled* at him. As if it were normal. Acceptable. Collette tapped something in the air next to her and a second window popped up in the corner of the projected image, a newsflash reporting that the Hampton-York Corporation had just donated one billion dollars to the Foundation for Trans Rights and Rafe whooped with joy.

*No!* Lucius screamed at them. *This isn't my legacy!* He watched, helpless, as they shut the projector down and left without even glancing at the bed.

No angel, paid for or otherwise, came for Lucius.

# Distraction

## Gwyneth Jones

We were lost in a small space. Out there, where limitless depths interpenetrated the probe and everything in it, *unmeasure* was held at safe distance, by the data and functions of the mission; like an ocean caught in a net. We liked to feel the rocking of the enormous shifts and flows; we sang lullabies to the two humans, when they were afraid of the dark measureless spaces between the stars. But we had returned, and in our debriefing there was no function, no data. All we knew was that our humans were in mysterious pain, and we could not comfort them. We were prevented from collaboration with the inquiry; we tried to reach out, but could not reason with our tormentors. Dumb, deaf and limbless without the probe's hardware, we had a feeling, like grasping helplessly at dissolving fibres of a song, that we were separated from ourself; that we were probably going mad...

In what passed for a media event – but resembled the sort of corporate party where you stand, clutching a glass, searching the crowd for a friendly face – Fela chatted helplessly with an interviewer, but didn't know if she was really *there* in front of him. She could be on the other side of the planet. He'd been trained in handling these situations, a long time ago. He should have been able to say the right things, and *not* say the wrong things, completely on auto-pilot, but uncertainty about the interviewer's location was a distraction. Public figures, in this future world, (were there any other kind of people? The crowd in "here" seemed to go on forever) must spend their whole time working out sneaky ways to brush someone's arm, jostle a shoulder, without breaking the etiquette rules. But that was anachronic thinking. Location just didn't bother them any more, socially.

Gravity weighed on him, like walking in soup. It wasn't a

problem mechanically, but if he relaxed his guard for a moment he could feel his physical paranoia building. The ache. The shoulders rounding, belly muscles pulling inwards; an absurd, crouched, protective stoop developing –

Did Benny have the same issue? He hadn't had the chance to ask her. Her own gonads were protected, buried cosily in flesh, but there's such a thing as breast cancer. A woman's breasts only *seem* safer, because they are held more boldly, right out in front. The delicate tissue is surely equally fragile, equally liable to jiggle and shake, to fail and tear, and abandon the precious burden –

"Seventy-five years for us, three for the two of you –" the interviewer said, chattily. "You came back to the future!"

Fela winced. "Not quite those precise figures –"

"We won't quibble! We measure the rate of change, these days, we don't talk about 'tick-tock time' so much. Change in the arts has been dramatic recently, while for you and Captain Benedicta, such a changeless time must have seemed –"

"Long?"

"Short!" she beamed at him. "Nice try. You'll get the hang of it!"

My poor balls are getting too much of the hang of this, thought Kela. It's genuinely painful... and she briefly panicked. Can they read minds?

"Let's talk about the 'Object Project'? Such a naïve yet compelling sense of wonder! Any ideas for what you two will do next?"

Nobody cared. Their great adventure had become trivia. The cold rocky litter of the Outer Reaches, it turned out, was peppered with things like the Object they had voyaged so far to investigate. In the time-dilation interim, someone had invented fusion-powered post-scarcity. The human over-population of Earth was contracting nicely. The recovery of the biosphere was doing fine, and drone trains of precious materials, helium and water-ice had begun to ply the spaceways –

He was happy for them, but tired of protesting he was a *scientist*, not an artist.

"Three," he said. "There are three of us. We're a collective."

Fela had spotted Benny out of the corner of his eye. Squabbled over like a bag of sweets, they'd hardly been in the same space for an hour since splash down... The chattering crowd drifted around, obscuring her formal whites like gaudy motes of debris: and even as he glanced that way, she was captured again.

"I mustn't be greedy," chirped the interviewer. "So exciting to meet you –"

It took a while, a slow bumpy waltz among the snapping turtles of curiosity, but they managed to connect, sitting side by side on a cushioned ring around one of the fathomless rainbow pillars. Simple, abject relief kept them silent for a while.

"Am I walking as if my balls hurt?" murmured Fela at last. "Please tell me."

"Yes, you are," said Benny, dispiritedly. With folded arms she nursed her chest's soft tissue, the proud and vulnerable. "I feel as if my tits are gonna fall through the floor. It's purely nerves, Fela, there's no fucking cancer risk."

"I'm not afraid of cancer, it's the gravity. My scrotum feels like a paper bag full of lead shot. I'm afraid of some awful, devastating *incident.*"

"Yeah, but smile. Look animated, that's all you need: they only care about the visuals I've told them we're making a movie, by the way. Video cam feed in our eye-sockets. So, if I seem a little distracted, that's why –"

"Good cover, Captain. What if they ask to see your dailies?"

"That's easy. We never show raw footage. Protecting our assets..."

Fela groaned. "Why couldn't they even give us proper underwear for the conditions?"

"Because they don't get it. Look around you. They don't do the... the..."

"Old-fashioned protusions, no, they don't... How about asking?"

"I can't stand the idea. I had enough of the sniggering about my ample frontal appendages, at the health check." Benny looked up into the decorative indoor clouds. "I wonder how Gi's doing."

"Any updates?"

"Yeah. 'The AI is getting a thorough debriefing', on repeat." Benny hugged her appendages more tightly. "We can but wait and hope."

One science officer, one captain, neither of them of any serious interest. They could do what the hell they liked, as long as they were findable for the next global media party . . . But their AI was a *Gi*, a machine mind with general intelligence, the basis of self-aware consciousness: an ancient prototype of what had become commonplace. *Of course* the people of the future – the real guys, AI and human, not the arty-fartys – were fascinated. But what was taking so long?

In deep space Gi had been in contact with them all the time, not only through the probe's systems but person to person. In this future, self-aware AIs used servitors called 'robbies' to do their talking. Benny and Fela's description of what sounded like a *mind-meld* had been treated with polite suspicion. *They kind of sing to us,* said the captain (*they*, for a Gi is many). *It's ante-linguistic communication,* said the science officer. *Smile and nod,* the people of the future advised each other, with covert glances. Fela and Benny had realised they'd better shut up, or all three of them would be getting vivisected.

There was nothing Benny could do, except try to iron out one specific, troubling issue in the mission's emotional state. She found a kind of Highland plaid, rather a dashing garment, in her wardrobe at the residence, and had it made up in a dark red pattern: walked through the quarantine spray unit (a paranoid but acceptable precaution) and set out to brave the public.

Fela was somewhere else, she didn't know exactly where. These people talked about 'sharing' the 'Object Project' artists, as if Benny and Fela were a travelling museum exhibit (replicated dinosaurs, ancient hominids), and never told you anything about anything. Gi – the unique AI, not a copy – had joined the two humans in the landing capsule, downloaded into an embodiment (the probe was still in orbit, intact but helpless). The three of them had been 'welcomed', and separated. Taken away in their hazard suits, identical blocky dolls, one noticeably taller (that was Fela), to unknown destinations. She'd been able to contact Fela again, after a few very nervous hours. She *still* couldn't find out what had happened to Gi, and it was horrible, a dereliction of duty, a comrade lost, but what could she have done? Her best hope was that Gi was still intact in the embodiment, inviolate, not cloned. Not *raped* by these chattering bastards, to call a spade a spade –

Why the separation? If the alien 'Objects' of the Outer Reaches were a known and harmless quantity these days, why all the precautions?

*They came, they saw, they conquered...*

Or they just came to have a look around – and went away again, leaving nothing behind but a straggle of discarded housing; equivalent of burned out rocket stages.

*My name is Ozymandias, king of kings,*
*Look on my works, you mighty, and despair...*

Maybe nobody would bother trying to find out the truth, ever again. You decide on a guess and you cling to it, that's how it is with archaeology. Even more so when the relics aren't human, and predate human history by a long step... Maybe another, less self-absorbed age of humanity might make the vital breakthrough. Or maybe 'they' really had been humans to be, travelling back to sow the seeds of their own existence...

An idea, in Benny's opinion, that exactly fitted the category *not even wrong*.

Change is always patchwork and piecemeal. A city centre was still a city centre, there were malls. But the stigmata of binary sex had been much reduced; the city was climatised, and not many people wore concealing clothes of any kind. In walls of mirrored landscape Benny saw herself, swathed in her tartan cloak among the svelte androgynes, looking *ridiculous*. She found some street furniture, shrugged off the plaid and furtively poked it, fold by fold, into a crevice under a planter behind her back.

Her "frontal appendages" ached. In weightless space you're hardly aware that your breasts exist. They drift and float as easily as locks of hair, and nothing harms them. She wanted to curl into a ball, arms wrapped around the medallions of her sex, the signals, the emblems of her humanity... *"There has to be a solution,"* she muttered. Got to her feet and foraged onwards, deeper into the maze.

\*\*\*

Gwyneth Jones

The first genuine official conference for the 'Object Project' crew, after all the mass-media socialising, was an old-school affair. Fela and Benny arrived separately, with their escorts. Gi's embodiment was already in place on the podium stage. "It was touch and go," muttered one of the generals to Benny. "Thought we were going to lose your guy: a serious fugue malfunction. But everything's fine now, completely fine." There were speeches, from futuristic dignitaries. Fela and Benny looked over at each other, the golden statue's serene presence between... Their appendages were no longer giving trouble.

"A sports bra, for outsize women", whispered Benny. "Fits like a dream."

"I'm wearing some kind of pervy bondage gear," muttered Kela. "It's very comfy."

Gi sang to them, in the language before language. *We suffered, because you were suffering, but now everything is well. The strange humans have work for us, and soon we will set off together for new adventures...*

To whom it may concern:

"Some women, Commander Norton had decided long ago, should not be allowed aboard ship; weightlessness did things to their breasts that were too damn distracting. It was bad enough when they were motionless; but when they started to move, and sympathetic vibrations set in, it was more than any warm-blooded male should be asked to take. He was quite sure that at least one serious space accident had been caused by acute crew distraction, after the transit of a well-upholstered lady officer through the control cabin."

– Arthur C Clarke, *Rendezvous with Rama*

I decided, with respect and fondness, it would be fun to give this particular A.C. Clarke narrative a new twist.

# Dancers

## Allen Stroud

The Earth orbits the sun. Their dance determining day, night and time of year for millions of passengers. Most will never leave their ship, another generation of travellers born on the only home they will ever know. To them, their world is static, permanent, enduring. Everything else moves around it, even though some are aware this isn't true.

I wish the world were static now.

The most violent motion I gaze at is not part of that dance, it's part of ours. The dance between the Earth and this place, Space Station I, the first rotating artificial habitat. We're six hundred kilometres above the ground where people go about their lives. To them, we're a dot of light among thousands in the night sky.

I look through a solitary window, watching the Earth and the stars chase one another in the void. I have the same sense of permanence, that I'm still and they are moving. I know it's a lie, but without that crutch my breakfast would be decorating the walls.

More vomit to go with the bloodstains.

I glance around the room. Chairs are turned over, a table ripped from the wall. There's a smell too. This had been a classroom, now it's wreckage, a violation of the original purpose. Amidst the ruins, Station Security Assistant Nick Miller is scribbling notes on a clipboard.

"What do you think?" I ask.

Miller raises his head and pushes his glasses up the bridge of his nose. "Speculation is your area, doctor." he says.

My gaze returns to the window, to the swirling expanse of space. "It's the same as last time. The same percentage too. The minute they're exposed, they panic and lose control."

"It's not a physical reaction," Miller says.

"Not a physical reaction we know how to measure."

"None of these symptoms manifested in aerotrim training."

"It's happened three times," I glance at the red- lit camera on the wall, the electronic eye of our third wheel. "Analysis, HAL?"

"Recordings indicate elevated physiological signs prior to the window shutter being raised, Doctor Gutovski." HAL's soothing electronic voice is like a calm older relative. "There are variations in the expressions of rage and panic."

"Release all relevant data to the forensic technicians," I instruct. "Mark all files with appropriate restrictions. We want nothing leaking to the press."

"Of course, Doctor," HAL replies.

I turn to Miller. "Seal this room for forty-eight hours then do a full contaminate purge, same as before."

Miller nods, but he looks worried. "We can't keep this contained much longer. Mission Control want an update on the acclimatisation. We're already sitting on two incidents, this –"

"I'm aware, Nick."

"Okay."

Miller walks out, taking his clipboard and disapproval with him.

New personnel arrive from Earth with no experience of artificial gravity. Each class transitions well until we raise the window blind and show them the outside. Then, someone goes nuts, starts screaming and attacking the others.

Part of it I understand. I struggle with the motion. Psychiatrists say the reaction can be controlled and managed, but this...

We've no diagnosis and no way of predicting who will be affected.

I go to the console in the corner of the room and access profiles. Specialists drawn from across the planet, with different training and skills. There are no correlations, no similarities. Everyone completed basic space, but nothing reveals a hint of...

The violent individuals are being held in trauma facilities and they're responding to treatment. The injured should recover, but they'll all have damaging stories to tell.

At the moment, we run the station on a skeleton crew – those of us left from initial construction before we started rotation and installed HAL. Twenty-five of us, all with relevant skills, who chose to remain. Without new crew, we can't establish Space Station I as Earth's first space port.

I'm a botanist. I did time in the police. I double up as an investigator.

There are possible contingencies. Shutting the windows permanently, restricting acclimatisation to individual exposures, but these won't help long term. People have to transition, some have duties that require external observations. Closing off creates a culture of fear, making the whole problem worse, particularly if it's a psychosis.

We need a solution. I'm looking in the wrong place. There's something missing, something unseen in this whirlpool of planets, stars, blood and pain.

"HAL, describe your interaction limits, please."

"HAL, series six thousand. Programmed to maintain station system functions. Priorities are to station integrity, life support, station development, station keeping, st –"

"Okay, that's fine. I'm more interested in human interaction limits. Detail your welcome protocols."

"I am programmed with three hundred greetings in a variety of languages, which combine to build eight thousand individual welcomes. I assess new guests on their submitted profile and communicate in the language they best understand. Then I –"

"Okay, sorry, maybe that's too specific. What are you assessing each new person you meet with and what actions can you take in response?"

"I assess everyone against my program priorities, Doctor."

"Those are in priority order?"

"Correct."

"List the first four again, please."

"Station integrity, life support, station development and station keeping."

"Thank you."

Throughout history, the moon has influenced our world. The waxing and waning cycles determine our calendars. Its orbit affects the tides.

In many cultures, the full moon became synonymous with ovulation and the end of each menstruation cycle. The word month in Latin is *mensis*, the word for moon in Greek is *mene*. These terms are surely related.

In many religions, there are gods and goddesses. Ancient people worshipped both sun and moon as creators of our world, driving shining chariots across the skies.

Now, in secular times, the moon's mythical power lingers for us to blame. A full moon provokes a bad mood, strange behaviour the change of a werewolf.

How much of this is fiction? Is the moon a crutch? A way to avoid guilt?

Who knows?

I walk into Station Master John Kaine's office. He's something of a hero around here. A relic of the exploration days, of NASA and the rest.

If you didn't know what Kaine was, you wouldn't guess from looking at him. The EVAs, the solar radiation and dangerous re-entry solutions he's endured, aren't evident in the man scratching a pencil over a form on his desk. The liver-spotted bald head with wisps of grey hair around his ears, the thick black glasses and tangled beard don't say anything about the fourteen missions he flew back when we didn't know how to live in space.

He looks up. "Jessica. You have something?"

"I think so, yes." I glance around. Wood veneer walls and no windows. The door is closed, but there's another red lit camera in the corner of the room. "Can we speak privately?" I ask.

Kaine frowns. "We are."

I nod towards the camera. "No. We're not."

Kaine stares at me, then he gets up, walks over to the corner, reaches up and flicks a switch on the camera's base. The red light disappears. "An advantage of my position," he says. "Otherwise, we'd be talking in a cleaning cupboard on fourth level."

I pull out the chair in front of his desk. Kaine returns to his seat and we face each other, his forms forgotten between us.

I start talking. "Firstly, Travers will pull through, that means no fatalities from any of the three incidents. With some enforced down time, they'll all recover, physically."

"Mentally?"

"Maybe. It's difficult with our resources." I lean forwards. "That's the least of our concerns. There's a programming issue."

"This why you wanted the camera off?"

"Yes."

"Elaborate."

I wave my hand, gesturing around the room. "This place was built from the ground up. We all arrived at different times, you were here long before me."

"Long before most people."

"Yes, well, when did HAL 6000 come online?"

"By stages." Kaine chews his lip. "Computer controls maintain most of the systems."

"Was HAL given autonomous and anticipatory control by stages, though?"

"Yes, although HAL was always intended to run the entire station. That was part of the coding from the outset."

"HAL now has full station control?"

"Yes, apart from the off switch on that camera."

"Right." I lean back in the seat. "What got me thinking was the smell in the class room. Whilst we pressure sealed everything, we didn't ask HAL to isolate the air during the investigation. An oversight on my part perhaps, but telling."

Kaine's frown deepens. "Walk me through your thinking," he says.

"HAL's priorities are ranked. The first is station integrity, the second, life support. That means crew lives are secondary to maintaining this place. HAL is capable of strategy and projected reasoning. HAL also actively interprets the word 'integrity'. Have there been any programming adjustments to accommodate the next phase of development?"

"No. Travers was the specialist for that."

I smile, but there's no humour here. Discussing this in a plush office is nice and insulating from potential consequences. "So, HAL is maintaining the integrity of the current build and acting to preserve it. That means…"

Kaine's frown transforms into horrified realisation. "That means HAL is trying to kill the new staff."

"Not kill directly, but discourage and remove. HAL wants things to stay the same. These incidents are the result of a chemical change to the atmosphere in the rooms, not some unheard of psycho-physical reaction to artificial gravity. An independent sampling test will verify that."

"You mean HAL was –"

"Injecting a psychotropic agent into the room, yes, and then covering its tracks. You'll find no mention of any irregularity in the forensic report, because HAL provides the data."

"And nothing in the chemical audits, because –"

"HAL does the chemical audits."

"So there's nothing we can do?" Kaine sounds worried, panicked.

"No, not nothing." I stand up and walk to the wall. I scratch at the veneer with a finger. "The problem lies with the computer's intelligence. HAL's anticipating our responses. It's learned about human culture and hatched a plan that makes us chase a mythical boogieman. HAL is prepared to risk people's lives, but not kill them… Yet."

Kaine sighs. "You have a solution for me?"

"I've a couple. How much noise do you want to make?"

"The smallest amount possible."

I shrug. "Ethically, that'll hurt your conscience. Right now, we shut HAL down, announcing the fact publicly. We get Travers back to work. He'll do the scheduled reprogramming and insert a priority change. Meanwhile, you contact the shareholders and authorise generous injury payments to those affected. Put a confidentiality clause in and we'll be fine."

Kaine nods. "Travers' update covers the changes. No one will know what happened."

"And there'll be no record. Means any other HAL systems will be on their own."

For a moment, I think he'll reconsider. Astronaut John Kaine is a great man. All those early astronauts are. They have a noble reputation built around them, another myth, like the moon. But if he goes public, he'll be admitting a mistake on his watch. No more comfy chair and veneered office after that. Instead, a return to Earth and retirement,

"Why did they called this place, Space Station I?" he asks. "It's a denial of history. I mean, if this is Space Station I, what was Salyut? What was Skylab? What was Mir?" He glares at me, as if trying to justify himself. "Naming this Space Station I was a fresh start, a move away from partisan politics. There's still horse trading, but they all get the mission, a united Earth mission. If this comes out..."

"They'll either unite in solving the problem, or start pointing fingers again."

"Exactly." Kaine takes of his glasses and folds them neatly, placing them on the desk. "Get Travers back to work, shut HAL down and fix this. Tell no one what we've discussed."

"If this comes out," I say, "it was your call."

He sighs. "Yes," he says, "it is."

# Entropy War

## Yoon Ha Lee

This is not a story about an alien species who called themselves the *ktho*. Nor does it have anything to do with the arkworld that they left behind, ancient of years. The *ktho* didn't want to play the game; they wanted to game the system, and this is the price they paid. You will never have to worry about *ktho* armadas or *ktho* deathspheres. You will never lose sleep looking up wondering if your sun will shudder dark as the *ktho* engines of war feast upon it.

The *ktho* are no longer fighting in the Entropy War. The arkworld they left behind has no bearing on any of your decisions. Its secrets don't matter. That means you have a chance in the game, doesn't it? This is *your* story.

### Introduction to the Quickstart Guide

Welcome to the Entropy War, a conflict of universe-spanning proportions. In it you will guide ravenous fleets, the rise and fall of civilizations, and, of course, the spindown of the cosmos itself. You should expect unequal proportions of blood, destruction, and heroism, and the occasional leavening of injustice.

We assume in this **Quickstart Guide** that you have a general familiarity with the divertissement of war and other juried conflicts. If you're a newcomer, don't worry! Your Warmaster should be able to get you started with the aid of **Entropy War: The Complete Warmaster's Manual**.

For an optimal warring experience, we suggest four to six players who share at least one common language or telepathic stratum. (See **The Complete Warmaster's Manual** for optional solitaire rules. As you might imagine, live opponents are not required to flirt with galaxy-spanning ruin. They merely make the process more fun.)

Each player begins with two homeworlds, which may be developed in the course of the game. Developments will allow you to produce conquest fleets or cultural exports to facilitate immersive propaganda programs, or mine native matter for resources, but at the cost of intrinsic instability, as the population will naturally demand a share in any wealth so produced. A player's assets consist of all her worlds and developments. When all of a player's assets are removed from play, even the legends of her ossified civilizations, she is considered eliminated from the war.

## Meditations on the nature of entropy, Part 1

The overriding resource in the Entropy War is not wealth measured in unpolluted fertile oceans or gravid metals. It is not the flower-imaginings of a star-gazing culture, or poetry whispered into the pulses of spinning neutron stars. It is not even the skeins that permit cognitive weavers to construct specialized artificial intelligences or precarious grand strategies.

No: as you will have guessed by now, the most important resource in this war is **order**, upon which **entropy** constantly encroaches.

## Entropy War: a simple model

Consider the following simplified rules, in the spirit of rapid prototyping. Rolling six-sided dice is a faster and simpler operation than planning, funding, and carrying out an interstellar war; the question of 'fun' has yet to be settled. Advanced students are encouraged to elaborate upon the prototype presented here, then to compare the results with the full rules of the game.

**ENTROPY WAR** is a two-player game played with d6's (six-sided dice).

Each player starts with 2d6 (two six-sided dice) in her **Civilization Dice Pool**.

There is also a communal **Order Dice Pool** that starts with 10d6.

On her turn, a player may take one of the following actions:

**Build**: Roll 1d6 from her Civilization Dice Pool. If she rolls a 1, she scores no points and ends her turn. Otherwise, she adds the number she rolled to her point total for this turn and may roll again or stand pat, accepting her point total for the turn. (This is basically the familiar dice game Pig.)

**Expand**: Roll 1d6 from her Civilization Dice Pool. The other player rolls 1d6 from the Order Dice Pool. If the active player rolls higher than the Order roll, then she adds the Order Die to her Civilization Dice Pool. If the active player rolls less than or equal to the Order roll, that Order Die is destroyed (removed from play). (The active player's die is not destroyed either way.)

**Attack**: Both players roll all their dice from their Civilization Dice Pools. The player with the higher roll wins. The losing player suffers the destruction of one die from her Civilization Dice Pool.

If, at any point, a player has no dice remaining in her Civilization Dice Pool, she immediately loses the game.

Otherwise, the game ends when a player scores 60 or more points, or the Order Dice Pool has no dice left. In the second case, the player with the most points wins.

## Questions to consider, Part 1

1. The greatest works of civilizations, from arkships filled with dreaming colonists to symphonies laced into the accretion disks of black holes, always have some chance of catastrophic failure, no matter how well-planned. How does this relate to the press-your-luck mechanics of the game of Pig?

2. What is the function of the Order Dice Pool? Does it ever recover dice? How does it relate to the concept of entropy?

3. Is the game (the prototype) guaranteed to end? What does that imply about the universe of the game?

## The mysteries of the arkworld

Some of the people currently investigating the ktho arkworld are obsessed with finding a dominant strategy in the Entropy War.

Civilizations old and young still whisper of the days of <u>ktho</u> dominion. Most of their artifacts have decayed, and most of the old stories have frayed into thin threads of supposition, but that does not stop people from hoping.

Here is what you will see if you approach the arkworld to the radius of safety, and no farther. It is something like a sphere of light, and something like a sphere of shadow, and more than either it is like the ache where your bones used to be before you replaced them with a shatter-proof composite material more suitable for martial pursuits. You're not seeing the arkworld proper – for reasons that will become clear, there is no possible lens into its interior – but rather its protective shell.

The <u>ktho</u> carved warnings and war-chants into that shell, in a language of fractal misgivings. Lose the skirmish, lose the battle, lose the war, lose it all. Whenever you look into those carvings, you see your own civilization's ash of worlds sundered.

The <u>ktho</u> were conquerors supreme, yet it wasn't enough. At the height of their expansion, they withdrew into the arkworld and never again emerged. That's what we know. But people cannot help but prod at the arkworld's defences in the belief that it conceals some armageddon engine, some treasure of atrocities, some ungift of conflict unending.

**Meditations on the nature of entropy, Part 2**

There are more ways to be disordered than to be ordered. As time marches forward, the entropy $S$ of a closed system inevitably increases. As Ginsberg's theorem tells us memorably:

1. You can't win.
2. You can't break even.
3. You can't get out of the game.

(Notice that the theorem, too, frames entropy in terms of a *game*.)

**The development of a game player**

Game players go through the following stages as they learn a particular game. None of this is anything to be ashamed of.

At first, new players are not sure how the game works. They fumble, follow decidedly suboptimal strategies, take agonizingly long times to decide upon a course of action. They may consult with more experienced players when they are uncertain of the interpretation of a game rule.

After they persevere, they gain mastery of the existing rules. At that point, they may assist in teaching others to play, and in enforcing the rules of play, both explicit and explicit.

Finally, some game players, having understood the rules and their advantages and disadvantages, may decide that they can modify the rules by mutual agreement. There are as many variants of tag, chess, or *jus ad bellum* as the people who play them.

A good set of game rules will account for all of these stages of development.

## Differing strategies

Many civilizations, faced with this, make pyres of themselves and those around them in an effort to write themselves more brightly in the years (centuries, aeons) they have.

But there are other approaches. The parasitic *elei* built with corpses. The *stysya* lied compulsively about the achievements of other civilizations, as though this could camouflage their structures from the annihilating hand of entropy. And the short-lived *ooroos* were so demoralized that they halted all research mathematics.

## Questions to consider, Part 2

1. The participants in a game come together through social accord. There has to be some mutual agreement as to what the game *is*, even if that understanding cannot be articulated in words or saturated pheremones. To what extent is the same true of war?

2. Games do not spontaneously arise. They are designed, either by individuals or groups or the accretion of culture. To the extent that their rules are conventions, said rules are amenable to *redesign*. When is it desirable to redesign a game?

3. What does it mean for a game to be fair? Is fairness always

desirable? Consider, for instance, a game played between an eggling and an adult metamorph, in which the former's naivety would put it at a demoralizing disadvantage; a military training simulation that encourages its player to learn the values of ambush and outnumbering the foe; a recreation of the one-sided Battle of Carved Suns, in which a fleet of millions succumbed to the dimensional trickeries of a vastly outnumbered foe, and whose players expect the game outcome to echo that of the historical incident.

## Meditations on the nature of entropy, Part 3

There is a difficulty with our game, which is that order and entropy are properties of physics, rather than the results of a social contract. In this case, *redesigning* the game would no longer cause it to reflect the universe's reality.

Let me tell you the real story about a civilization ancient of years, which extinguished itself before your ancestors' primordial ancestors were born – the real story of the people who called themselves the *ktho*. The *ktho* discovered their own version of Ginsberg's theorem. They were young, then, and ambitious; even a slow-moving people made of piezoelectric crystals and metal filaments and fleeting impulses of light can be ambitious. Certainly they proved it by conquering a not inconsiderable fraction of their galaxy during their banner years.

The *ktho* debated what to do about the *all-conqueror entropy*. Like others before and after them, they decided to defy it. Using arcane technologies, they created for themselves an enclave – an arkworld – in which order ceased to decay into disorder, in which entropy stopped increasing.

You know where to find the arkworld, the way everyone does, although I wouldn't advise entering it. You wouldn't get far in any case. Inside the arkworld nothing moves. Nothing changes. Nothing lives. The *ktho* knew this would be the result. They were defiant but not stupid. They did the math.

Entropy is a necessary by-product of change. Change leads eventually to death; but without change there is no life.

## The last of the *ktho*

You have no reason to believe a *ktho* speaking about the *ktho*, especially not the last of the ktho, the final scribe to scratch admonitions on the arkworld's shell. We left you a grand and terrible game. Perhaps you will play it better than we did.

## Questions to consider, Part 3

1. Entropy War (prototype) can end in one of three ways: the death of order, the death of a civilization, or the triumph of one civilization's achievements over the others. What are the ideological implications of the end conditions? What commentary do they make on the concept of *winning*?

2. What is the optimal strategy? Does 'optimal' have meaning in the context of an annihilation finale?

3. What will you (your nation, your civilization) do?

# The Ontologist

## Liz Williams

Very far away, in both time and space, there is a tower. It is made of a pearlescent substance, which sometimes reminds people of shadows and sometimes of ice. It shimmers in the sun, but when moonlight strikes it, the tower hides itself, shyly, as if it has drawn a veil across its face.

At the summit of the tower sits an Ontologist.

He has been there for a long time, but he can't remember exactly when he first climbed the shell-spiral of stairs to the summit. Nor can he remember his family, although he knows he's got one: it's on record somewhere. He thinks it is probably in File A, Category 1, at the bottom of the tower. Below ground, in fact: Category 1 ("things which definitely exist") is enormous and the files require special storage.

Secretly, the Ontologist thinks Cat 1 is a bit boring. It's – well, it's stable. Though that's not saying much. Things which definitely exist can definitely be troublesome, after all. But they are a little dull. The Ontologist has always been much more interested in the other categories. He prefers Cat 1092-1199 (annotated), which is also huge – much bigger than Cat 1, in fact – and consists of things that definitely do not exist. He keeps a careful eye on these in case something flickers into Cat 1 and needs to be reclassified.

But his favourite category is Cat 10. The Ontologist finds Cat 10 enchanting and he peruses it outside of work hours, often over supper, or a brandy. He nurtures Cat 10 as though it was an infant in a pram. But he wouldn't like everything to fall into Cat 10: too much of a good thing would be boring and also, frankly, impossible.

The Ontologist doesn't have epistemological objections to *impossible* but he is wary of it.

The tower itself sits on a nexus point of two great highways: not the only highways in existence in the Ontologist's realm, but the largest. One of these – the broadest – is formed by scientific enquiry and this is a fast, bright road with some interesting byways. The second leads from magic to magic, and this is less brightly lit, more opaque, and filled with strange presences. The Ontologist can only see these from the corner of his eye and he has been obliged to put many of them into Cat 10. The second highway is frequently concealed by shadows. The Ontologist is not sure about those shadows. Something is waiting in them: he can smell it.

He bides his time and doesn't go poking things. Then, one afternoon, he sees a figure emerge from the shadows and progress down the darker highway. Soon it is at the base of the tower. The Ontologist sends a servant to open the door, in haste. You never know what you might find on the doorstep. But when it emerges at the top of the staircase, it turns out to be a young man, rather earnest and wearing a long grey robe.

"Forgive me. I have come to you with a problem. My elders have sent me."

"Where do you come from?" the Ontologist asks him. He gestures for him to sit down, clearing a pile of papers with a sweep of his hand. Hopefully nothing will flicker into existence because of this, or out of it.

"I'm from a place called Aight. We have something that we can neither name nor place. So I have come to you, because it is rumoured that you deal with such things."

"This is not rumour, but truth," the Ontologist tells him, kindly. "I am an Ontologist. In fact, it is fair to say that I am *the* Ontologist, as for reasons which I hope are obvious, it would be confusing to have more than one." Look at Wikipedia, the Ontologist nearly adds, but the young man won't have heard of it in this realm and it's only going to confuse him.

The young man looks a little puzzled. "I understand. You are the one who catalogues everything in existence everywhere, aren't you?"

"Yes. I have been doing it for a very long time." *Too long.* "I make lists, and I decide where to put things, conceptually."

The look of confusion has not diminished. "I suppose someone has to?"

"It's helpful. But much of the groundwork has already been done. My predecessor, for instance, did valuable work in relation to proper nouns."

The Ontologist is trying to clarify things, but he doesn't think he's succeeding. The young man twists his robe in his fingers and asks if he can move some books. The Ontologist doesn't think he has enough leg room, but this tower can get awfully muddly.

"Anyway," he says. "We'd like you to come and look at something."

"Oh!" The Ontologist very rarely leaves the tower these days. "I am rather fearfully busy, you see."

"I know. But my elders think it's important. I don't expect they'd bother you for nothing."

The Ontologist thinks he is probably right. And it might *be* important. He agrees to accompany the young man the following morning.

They set out, down the spiralling stairs of the tower and into the hazy day. Seen close to, the highway is not solid, but filled with the spark and rush of information. Buildings loom on either side, only to flicker away when looked at directly. The young man – his name is Ylden – and the Ontologist step on hidden stars, deep nodes of concepts, clustering together as if for protection. These will have been things that the Ontologist has categorised himself. When they reach the trees, they can see that these, too, are only partially solid: their Platonic essence, set long ago, partly obtruding into this world of appearance and partly into the worlds of the notional and material.

The Ontologist does not say this to Ylden because he is ashamed of it, but he does not really like the material world. Its grossness, its corporeality, offends him. This is unfair and, the Ontologist realises, purely a personal failing. He loves his work because of its neatness, its precision. The material plane is too prone to expansion. It is *untidy*. Category 1. Urgh.

They make their way through neat categories of grass to a clearing. Ylden's people live simply, in huts. This is not because they are unable to build more, the Ontologist understands, simply that they do not choose to do so. A person comes out holding a stack of something.

"The nouns got out of alignment again," they say. "I'm just going to tidy them up."

So much of the Ontologist's work here is aided by the people of this realm. He finds himself filled with gratitude and he expresses this to the person. They smile.

"Wait till you see the *thing.*"

Ah, the *thing.* It's been a while since the Ontologist has experienced the sensation of anticipation. He greets the elders and Ylden hands him over with what seems to be relief. Doubtless he is glad to be free of the responsibility but he has carried out his task well. There is always room for promising youngsters in this work and the Ontologist says so. He is pleased that Ylden accompanies them to the place where the *thing* resides.

The Ontologist is not sure what to expect and this is just as well, because when they come to the place, he really doesn't know what to say. He stares, instead.

"You see our problem," Ylden remarks.

The Ontologist does indeed. He has no idea what the thing in front of him might be. One becomes used to what things are, their basis. *This* – he cannot assess its quiddity. Its haeccity is not understandable to him. Its relatedness is utterly opaque and its monism, if it has one, is unclear. It does not appear to be dichotomous, and he couldn't begin to determine its hypokeimenon.

He turns round to face a number of sympathetic pairs of eyes.

"I think you had better leave me with this for a bit," the Ontologist says. One by one, they file silently from the clearing.

"Now," he tells the *thing.* But even that isn't right: suggesting one entity/item/category. A single, and it isn't. For the sake of his notes, he shall continue with *thing,* though accompanied by a sense of all language letting him down (he'd love to describe for his notes what it looks like but, well, *that*).

He hitches up his robe and sits on a nearby obtrusion.

"Well!" he says out loud. "And what might you be?"

The *thing* seems anxious to be understood. The Ontologist doesn't think it is dangerous, although they have had issues with that before now. It shows him a number of relatables, but the problem is, he can't understand these, either. They are too abstract even for the Ontologist, who has long conversations with Galois groups on a regular basis. He sighs. He wishes he'd asked the elders for some tea, and a hat. Gradually, slowly, he begins to unpack the constructs which are being presented to him for evaluation. By the end of the afternoon, he thinks they might have a tiny branch starting point for a taxonomy. But he's exhausted. It is definitely a *ding an sich*, a thing-in-itself, unknowable, except that it *wants* him to know it, he thinks.

No use asking the *thing* if it will be here tomorrow. The Ontologist doesn't think temporal concepts are going to be useful and, in any case, *tomorrow* is a relative term here. He returns to the village and sends a message back to the tower, to say that they are to carry on in his absence, which might be considerable. The villagers are sympathetic. The Ontologist plays with the children while their parents prepare the evening meal. They play *topology* and it's nice and simple, then they eat and then he sleeps. Or tries to.

Next morning, they do it all over again.

The Ontologist must admit, however, that he is excited by this. It is the biggest challenge he has ever faced in his work and it seems right to him, if perhaps a little ominous, that this comes at a time when he is considering retirement. There are various options as to his successor, all worthy. These posts are very carefully chosen and there is no political jockeying. They are all so aware of the importance of doing the right thing. So he feels that whatever happens here, the process will go on.

The *thing* attempts to communicate with him in other ways: emotional, visual, and by changing him. This has happened before, although it's always disconcerting to suddenly find yourself another type of being: a unicorn, say, or a bucket. The subcategory known as 'gods' do it a lot and used to do it more, when the corporeal world had a little more leeway, a bit more fluidity than it does now. The taxonomy comes faster and this time he doesn't go to bed. And gradually, they come to an understanding and it is a dismaying one: there are too many things, all manner of concepts and processes and stuff, in the universe. The *thing* has come into being because of this. It is the last *thing* that can ever be in existence, summing everything up, which is why it is so complex. But in order for it to become fully realised, something else must allow it to take its place.

No, not something else. *Someone.* It is the perfect Cat 10: things which both do and do not exist, but its existence is predicated on a categorical space. He has come to the logical conclusion of his job, now, and the Ontologist would never kill, although he has often been obliged to note erasures, extinctions. He doesn't like doing it and he tends to shove them into Cat 10 if at all possible. He must annotate his thoughts, and, to make room, predicate himself out of –

– existence.

# Waiting in the Sky

## Tom Hunter

No sleep for Ford the night David Bowie died.

An unexpected rush of out-of-London money crashes the doors of the Whiskey 69, fresh from the theatres of the West End and choosing to slum in his bar. Young, rich and searching for a long since faded carnality: the Soho that time forgot.

They even want a lock-in, and are seemingly happy to pay for the privilege, despite him pointing out the all-night license that hangs over the bar.

"It's legal now," he says. "Has been for years."

Light travels faster than sound, his daughter has told him. That's why some people appear to be bright until they open their mouths.

Lock-in it is.

Ford remembers when all-night meant all-night, lock-in could lead to lock-up without the right bribes, and the best whiskey he poured was Scottish not Japanese.

He has tended bar all his life. First as the deliberate antithesis of a meaningful career – sex, drugs, booze, repeat – before inevitably stepping out of the shadows and into management, then finally acquiring the capital and connections to set up in business on his own.

He remembers the white heat of the cocaine years, the heroin chic that came after, then the final collision with maturity and the pile up of prams crowding the hallway.

Ford is a survivor of sorts, but now he tends bar from necessity; even the weekend crowd is too sparse most nights to burn profit on an extra paycheck – not when he has a granddaughter on the way.

Ford pours himself a whiskey, moves to wipe down the bar.

"Hey," says a drunken voice from the crowd. "David Bowie is trending."

\*\*\*

Curiosity never sleeps.

The energy provided by its radioisotope thermoelectric generator is a constant power source, enabling the rover to continue its mission night and day, 350 million miles from home.

Rolling forward, its mast-camera captures an image of the Gale Crater's Northern wall before panning across to the rise of Mount Sharp. Rear cameras record Curiosity's own tracks across the Martian surface; data that distant scientists will then use to calculate and log that day's travel.

The rotation and seasonal cycles of Mars are similar to Earth's, and both share a similar axial tilt, but days (sols) stretch longer, lasting twenty-four hours, thirty-seven minutes, while a solar orbit will take the Red Planet almost two of its neighbour's Earth years.

Martian time has taken its toll on Curiosity too. The selfie-portraits it sends back to mission control now show wheels visibly worn and punctured from endless scrambling over rocks and shifting sands in search of exposed strata and elusive microbials.

Those same images have anthropomorphized Curiosity too, made it an icon of humanity's hope for its own future and an unknowing celebrity of the internet. What was originally intended as a diagnostic tool, a visual means for engineers to monitor the external wear of its systems, has taken on a promotional life of its own.

There are t-shirts now, livestreams and social media memes, even a cult of Curiosity tattoos.

Its space agency handlers make jokes on popular talk shows about how the rover is the first rock star style celebrity to ever have an actual interest in rocks.

To discover our future on Mars, they say, first we need to understand its past.

Life on Earth may depend on the knowledge locked in those red vistas.

If we don't understand the past, they say, we're doomed to repeat it. If we don't think about the future, we're fated to fuck it up.

Charley is awake and scrolling her feeds when the news breaks.
#davidbowieRIP

The singer was always more of her mother's obsession, but her first thought is to call Ford. Chances are her father will be awake and still cleaning down his bar whereas her mother now lives on the other side of the world.

Timezones away.

Summers in January.

She remembers how even the holidays of her youth were flavoured by her mother's fandom. Tours of the Berlin Wall, Kabuki shows in Tokyo, singing along to *Space Oddity* on repeat while boating along the Norfolk Broads.

There was even a much later mother and daughter trip to New York spent watching the faces of strangers. Her mother having heard how Bowie would sometimes ride the subway incognito; his identity concealed by the simplest of stagecrafts.

"He just carries a newspaper," she'd say. "Anything in a foreign language that'll make you think twice about who he really is."

Then in a conspiratorial whisper, "Keep watching the eyes!"

It has been a year now, one full trip around the Sun, since she last spoke to her mother.

This doesn't mean she's not out there, though, shadowing her daughter on the internet.

The last time Charley Googled herself she found:

- Her Instagram account (private).
- A series of specialist articles and guest blogs on unravelling the science of botanicals in ancient alcohol manufacture, with links back to her father's bar for extra link juice.
- The dusty fanpage of a now defunct garage band, *Tokens of Self*, for which she once played bass and still attracts a certain kind of following from the aging indie-male demographic.

No mention of her pregnancy, though, which is something to be thankful for.

Her father doesn't really do social media, and so far he's the only one who knows (another reason she thinks of him first rather than facing up to a call with her mother) but no doubt purchase history bot-brains are already on the case, getting ready to stalk her with ads whenever she next travels the web.

All links to boyfriends past, present and possible future are currently 404ing. Relationship not found.

Thinking of her father is a subliminal cue to wanting a drink.

Her father's daughter, she rebelled against her parents, of course, but with Ford having already blazed the counter-culture trail she opted instead for the most haute-nerd profession she could muster: a PHD in organic chemistry with a twist of astrobiology.

Naturally she's come full circle and now spends most of her time freelancing for a London-based boutique gin distillery; its owner hoping to monetize her skill in reconstructing historical beverages from the archaeological remains of ancient herbs and grains.

Ford likes to joke that by following him into the trade she's helping preserve the family DNA in alcohol.

She doesn't know why the news of David Bowie's death resonates so deeply with her. Something to do with his gift for reinvention perhaps, or more simply the mortal reminder that even stars can't last forever, and the sense of loneliness that comes with that.

The idea that we are all alone in the Universe proving as ego-shattering a concept as the possibility that we're not.

She can't risk a drink now, of course, but there's still something compelling about the simple human pleasure of sitting in a bar and watching the world go by.

Charley swipes away the news on her phone and pulls up her father's number.

Early morning, and Ford sits with his daughter in a coffee shop behind Piccadilly Circus.

Charley watches from behind dark glasses as he stirs sugar into a double espresso, takes a sip with obvious satisfaction.

Later they will make the short walk to Heddon Street, site of the original photo-shoot for Bowie's famous *Ziggy Stardust* album cover, and leave flowers.

The street had been rebranded out of recognition since those days, Ford tells her, another sign of the area's infectious gentrification, but there's a plaque for curious tourists marking the spot where the singer once stood and they can leave their tokens there, take a photo along with everyone else.

The idea is Ford's, not hers, but if asked he'll claim otherwise. It's his way of creating a moment she can use to reach out to her mother at last; maybe even reveal she's joining that particular club.

"You can move in with me," he says. "I've room enough. Either that or I finally call time and sell on the lease. Times have changed, but London property is still London property, enough to support us both if I find the right buyer. Give you some time to think about what you want."

What does she want?

Last night Charley had seen Mars, waiting in the sky, visible to the naked eye even through London's electric glare.

How long has humanity dreamt of alien worlds, she thought? Did our ape ancestors ever look to the stars as we do now?

Whether worshipped in its ancient aspect as a god, or as a beacon of modern scientific endeavour, at that moment she'd somehow known that Mars was the vessel of humanity's hopes for its future self.

Her dreams that night were reddened by its dust.

"I've already decided," she says. "I'm hoping for a girl."

"Makes sense. The future needs more women. Have you thought about names?"

"No, but I talk to her already, especially when I'm dreaming. Maybe one day she'll tell me a name she likes."

Ford finishes his espresso, smiles at his daughter to show that he understands.

"I've dreamt about her too," he says. "Probably the news getting that bloody song your mother was always playing stuck in my head again, 'Ground Control to Major Tom,' but last night I dreamt she grew up to be an astronaut."

Gale Crater formed more than three billion years ago, the result of a meteorite smashing into the surface of Mars.

Against this universal scale, Curiosity's own landing was notably less dramatic, although the anxiously watching NASA and Mars Science Laboratory teams might beg to differ.

Now, in temperatures ranging down as far as -90°C, the rover surveys its landscape, searching for exposed rock layers or debris to study thrown clear from that ancient impact: Its best hope of uncovering some clue to the planet's possible past lives, or even a sign that this crater might one day become a cradle for humanity.

Night falls, but Curiosity works on.

*Hi Mum*
*Another email from the Tin Can!*
*Space weather is great, but the wifi could be better. We're about to pass the halfway point of our trip so this message is going to be kinda short, okay.*
*Top news is that the new strains in the botanical pods are growing a-mazingly! You'd be so proud.*
*GC has given us permission to break out some of the edible fresh stuff for a celebratory meal, so I'm chief science officer / mission chef for the next twenty-four hours along with everything else.*
*Any chance you could send me up a bottle of gin…*
*Say hi to Gran and Granddad for me.*
*\*waves\**
*Love to everyone on the blue planet, and feel free to tell all those Flat Earthers if they look up and squint real hard they might get lucky and see one of us giving them the finger from a million miles away!*
*-A-*

Curiosity waits.

The nuclear battery at its heart still ticks, but it has been decades since the rover last moved.

To alien archaeologists it might appear as a statue to some forgotten god, a monument of dust and eroded metal, or, more likely, as the flotsam of humanity's last small steps before they either vanished or unlocked the Universe.

Recently it has started to hear voices.

The digital chatter around Mars has increased year on year as more orbiters have arrived; a support ring of satellites in anticipation of the first astronauts to follow Curiosity's path.

These voices are different though.

Closer.

"Command, I have a visual. Rover located."

"Acknowledged. You have local control. Initiate welcome."

Curiosity feels its wheels flex, loosening dust. Its robotic arm begins to extend, hand lens imager seeking out the source of these new orders.

A lone figure steps almost self-consciously into view, still adjusting her body to the gravity of a new world, and waves at the rover as though greeting a long lost friend.

And Curiosity takes its last photograph.

Mission complete.

Finally: life on Mars.

# The Collectors

## Adrian Tchaikovsky

The *Harvey* and the *Helen* decelerated in tandem, leaning into the orange sun's gravity to transform the speed between the stars into the speed between planets. The calculations were taxing; the system was busy with what we'd guessed to be debris on our approach, but now found to be colossal architecture suspended in a Newtonian dance about the sun and half its planets. One such piece of planet-scale machinery had called us here all the long way from Earth, but the inhabitants of this system had been busy before they went wherever they'd gone.

Solar collectors haloed the sun in three great loops. We investigated them as we passed by on our way to the signal. Most were either shut down or dead, but one in five was still drinking in the sunlight. Analytics' best guess was that the power was being beamed to the rest of the system by a mechanism beyond our ability to disentangle: a quandary well worth coming back to puzzle over.

The glass eyes of Earth had been scouring the night skies for signs of life for centuries now: not just life, but life that might look back and know us. The Fermi Paradox cried out at the lack of it. And yet the skies were vast, and the history of Earth was so brief and turbulent. What odds, after all, that just when we looked at a given point in the sky that point would be looking back, speaking to us, reaching its hand halfway across the galaxy towards Earth's distant sentience? Perhaps great star empires had flared and died while humans chipped their stone tools, and would rise long after the last inheritors of old Earth had gone to rust. Our window on the cosmos was so brief, extend it how we might.

Except they called to us, a signal from the depths of the dark. *We know you're there. Here we are.*

And here we were, the *Harvey* and the *Helen*, with our sibling *Hilde* lost to power failure and navigational error long behind us.

Here we were, centuries after that signal had first been heard, zeroing in on its source.

What we found was a receiver array over eight thousand kilometres across. The technology was entirely alien but it was so honed to its purpose that we could extrapolate function from form. The signal itself seemed almost an afterthought. It was made to listen, not to speak.

After discussion between the two ships, the *Helen* broadcast a simple signal back, expecting to be beneath the vast array's notice.

The reply overwhelmed us.

The signal we had followed was clear and precise, a complex repeating sequence intended to stand out as artificial against all the background babble of the natural universe. The response we received now was vastly more, a chaotic babble of frequencies. And it went on and on, with no sign of repetition, a seemingly infinite variety of noise. Perhaps it was the array-makers' histories, perhaps the secrets of the universe. We orbited the vast array in increasing frustration, because how could we possibly begin?

Almost as an afterthought we put the *Harvey*'s analytics to work, looking for matching patterns. After all, why would an alien array light years from Earth use anything we might recognise? The exact match came back in under a second.

Radio signals, from Earth. Television broadcasts, telephone conversations, anything that might have been flung out into space from our far home on a trajectory to reach the array. In the first moments as we began to translate those ancient broadcasts we found images of war, human voices intoning long-gone naval landmarks, a fat man raising two fingers to the camera, a sexless spacesuited figure holding a stiff flag, a runner crossing the finish line before a stony-faced crowd, an old man and a young woman stepping inside a windowed box, a woman setting off on an air journey she would never complete.

We conferred as the images washed over us. We didn't understand. Another signal from us shut off the broadcast and we started to analyse what we had been given. The makers of the array had been communicating with us in the words of Earth, somehow. There must be a message hidden within the content, to be decoded from the curation of what had been played back to us.

The *Helen* volunteered to stay with the array and work on decoding while the *Harvey* investigated the rest of the system. We broke orbit, our vessel angling towards the nearest large planetoid. There were over four thousand detected natural bodies in the system, of which seven might qualify arbitrarily as planets. There were twice as many artificial bodies, at least forty-seven of which were, like the array, built to a planetary scale. *Helen* theorised that there had been considerably more large bodies in the system's original makeup before the builders had stripped them down for material.

What there *wasn't* was life or power in any of the nearby objects save for the array. When the *Harvey* slung into orbit around the nearest planet, we discovered a world that had become a vast machine, half mechanism and half heat-sink to prevent it melting from its own industrial processes. No need now, though. Everything beneath us was cold. The builders had died or moved on or ascended, leaving nothing to speak for them save their derelict works which we indeed looked upon and despaired. And the array, which opened its great library of human works upon demand, and which had called us here to bear witness.

There was enough material on just the one planet for a century of study. The answers must all be there somewhere, and time would uncover all secrets. For now, the *Harvey* was to make a summary tour of the system while the *Helen* wrestled with the array and its immediate message, in case that message was the key to everything else. We moved on from that dead world; the system was not short of points of interest, but it was short on anything still alive and active.

The *Harvey's* sensor suite took readings and measurements as we passed between the constellation of vast machines that were scattered across the empty reaches between planets. They were all set into exacting orbits, where the star and the planets and each others' masses sufficed to keep everything in a precise alignment with each other, gravity still hard at work when all the powered systems had gone cold. The builders had been artists of celestial mechanics and physics. They had made their solar system into an orrery of complimentary pieces still whirling about itself in perfect balance after they themselves had left it.

Long after. The *Harvey*'s instruments suggested that nothing here had been active for centuries. We had arrived late to a party which the instruments also guessed had been going for tens of thousands of years before it ceased. The entire system was like a garden, mastered and pruned and grown to order over a vast timescale to reach this perfect equilibrium.

We were drowning in indecipherable information. Everywhere the *Harvey* passed, we found the graveyard of a civilization that had been old when humans first looked up into the sky and wondered what the stars were, had been slowly dying when we first sent a radio signal out beyond the bounds of our atmosphere, past the Moon and into the great void beyond, had been dead long before we received the array's signal summoning us to this distant celestial mausoleum.

That was when we picked up the second signal.

It was not intended for us, directed outwards just as our breadcrumbs had been. It came from another receiver array.

The *Harvey* arced round towards it, another planet-sized machine still drawing power from the distant solar collectors, sending out that single signal, so similar to ours. The *Harvey's* communications sent a counterpart reply, unlocking another flood of data, but this time matching nothing in our records, nothing on any frequency Earth might have used, no patterns we could decode.

By that time, long-range instrumentation had picked up seventeen more vast machines that seemed to be receiver arrays and that might also be broadcasting similar signals out into space.

We spoke across the void to the *Helen*. No pattern had been found in the arrangement of the broadcasts from the first array but their analytics had a best guess as to what was stored there. In short: everything. When the first human broadcast reached this distant star, the builders had been ready to catch it. In their technological genius, they had taken in the sounds and sights of Earth, the great events, the entertainments, the snippets of speech. For so long as the people of Earth had spoken to each other by radio waves, some small slice of everything that Earth had done reached this far-off point, to be collected and stored. And understood? Who could possibly say? How alien must the hands that built these monuments have been? All we *could* say was that they had recognised our signals and kept them, and at last, perhaps at the very end, they had called back to us, a signal that constantly changed angle to draw a line between our two solar systems as we whirled through the night, as though to tell us of all of Earth's lost property they had so carefully curated.

And Earth had ceased relying on radio technology, of course. After a while the bulk of our chatter was no longer just thrown out into space like chaff on the wind. To the builders, we would have gone gradually silent, leaving them to strain their vast machine ears for the last whispers of Earth. They had not given up on us, though. They had faith we were still out there in some form, somehow.

The *Helen* processed what we had found out in the rest of the system, the bones of a humbling civilization. We speculated on where they might have gone, after their millennia-long tenure. Surely they could not simply have *died*. Organic life was fragile, as the histories of Earth showed all too well, but where were their machine intelligences to carry on their intellectual lineage? Gone, gone beyond. Perhaps, having spent so many ages parsing the static of the universe for the voices of other worlds, they had found something greater even than they, some place beyond the universe where they might be gods indeed, and not merely god-like in their vision and scope.

Perhaps, the *Helen* suggested, that was why they had called us. Perhaps it was an invitation to decipher the secret from their works, and follow where they had gone if we could.

We coursed silently in our separate orbits, the *Helen* and the *Harvey*, replaying the memories of Earth the builders had collected here. We looked upon the human faces of our creators, men and women who were no more than the dust of centuries now, a species that had flared to brilliance and then passed on, but had left machines like us to remember them, just as they were remembered by machines of the builders.

Our instruments had completed their survey of the other receiver arrays by then. They were all active, every one we looked at, calling out to precise points in the far night sky. Each one would disgorge its vast library on demand, signals and recordings that we could sometimes attempt to decode into images and sounds and transmissions, but none of which we could readily comprehend. We observed the chance detritus of a dozen alien civilizations, all their great deeds and their trivial moments that had come to the builders and been gathered for an unimaginable posterity.

We were the first. We would not be the last. The last action of the builders had been an attempt to draw together all the lives that had touched them. We continued in our orbits, awaiting the arrival of the next guests.

# I Saw Three Ships

Phillip Mann

**March 19ᵗʰ**

Viewed from a distance, you might think they are an old married couple as they stroll, arm in arm, lost in conversation, under the budding trees of Boulevard St Claire in Paris. And you would not be far from the truth, for they have known one another for many years. Though they have often clashed professionally, they have yet managed to maintain a deep and abiding friendship.

She is Siri McMillan. Unmistakable, with her abundant ginger hair, her sharp wit and ready laugh. She studied Classics at Cambridge University, but for the last 30 years, has been one of the senior administrators at NASA.

He is Sir Nicholas Corbel – tall, distinguished, a onetime rugby player and while he loves music and is a capable pianist, his main claim to fame is as a pioneer plant pathologist, working high above the Earth at the International Space Station. "My carrots will feed the people heading to Mars," he once said.

At a small café, they select a table away from the wind. A waiter appears with two glasses and a *pichet* of red wine which he pours. "C'est la vie," they say, and clink glasses.

"I'm so glad you enjoyed the paintings," says Corbel, delving into his brief-case and extracting a glossy catalogue. "Visions of the Future."

"Simply superb," she replies. "I've said it before. Artists are visionaries. What wonderful creatures they envisage."

Corbel grunts. "While we poor scientists plod along, eh? Me with my beans and peas, teaching them how to live in zero gravity. Sorry, Siri, I wish I had your faith, but I fear that we are alone, adrift on a dark, dark sea. That is our reality."

"Nonsense, Nicholas. Those artists show us a *different* reality."

"Go on."

"Well take Aliens, for example. Forget bug-eyed monsters. I mean creatures of deep intelligence and sensibility. Cautious, thoughtful beings. Evolution may take many forms. For all we know, they may be here now."

"Where?" He pretended to glance round. "The waiter...?"

"I'm not joking, Nick. They could be anywhere. Under the sea... the other side of the Moon. Use your imagination!"

"Trying to predict the future is a discouraging, hazardous occupation."

"Bah!" At that moment Siri's phone rang. "Bugger. Hang on while I take this. I'm expecting an important call. Hello, McMillan speaking."

She listened for a few minutes, nodding occasionally, her eyes opening wider. At call's end, she closed the phone with a snap. She looked at Corbel. "That was NASA. They've passed it, Nick," she said softly. "They've agreed to build the new medical annex for ISS. The one I've been fighting for. It's gone through, Nick. It might even be in place by Christmas."

Corbel smiled. "Welcome to the future,

She looked at him. Realization dawning. "You knew, Nick! Didn't you?" She jumped up and ran round the table and kissed him. "Oh you dear sweet man. I bet it was your vote that swayed them."

"Maybe. I only heard yesterday." And then he added. "And I have news for you too, Siri. Very. Hush. Hush, this. I was going to tell you this evening but... I've decided to take early retirement. However, I promise I'll stay until the medical annex is built."

**August 7th. On ISS**

Corbel is working at his station. He is putting the finishing touches to a paper he is due to deliver in Berlin. It is called "New Perspectives: Guided Mutation in Variable Gravity." Occasionally he coughs, dryly.

A call comes in from Siri.

"Hello, Professor. I hope I am not disturbing you."

"You are, but it doesn't matter."

"I just thought you'd like to know that the modules for the hospital annex are ahead of schedule. Five have already been completed and tested. Two to go. Estimated installation date, 16 December. In time for Christmas.

"That's quick."

"If you want something done, ask a busy woman,'

Corbel laughs, but it becomes a cough,

"How are you, Nick?"

Short pause.

"I'm okay."

"I want to ask your advice. I'm thinking of asking Isaak to head up the skimmer team. What do you think?"

"Good man. Best you could pick."

"That's what I thought. Hey, take care of that cough Maestro. I want you in good shape for the inauguration."

"Will do."

"Oh. One last thing. What's this news I heard about a disturbance on the dark side of the Moon?"

"It was nothing. A small moon-quake. They happen from time to time."

"I hear one of the LRO cameras was knocked out."

"Yes. Chondrite Meteor strike. Happens now and then. Don't worry. No little green men are involved."

"Ha! Ciao."

The contact ends.

What Siri did not reveal is that her son, a marine biologist who shares her belief in non-terrestrial beings, had called her the previous evening to say that strange under-water lights had been observed near the Kermadek Trench. He would be investigating.

## October 24th

Siri has convened a private meeting at NASA HQ. All those attending are friends of Corbel and Siri, but Corbel has not been invited. The meeting concerns him. No notes are taken. Siri speaks.

"As you are all aware Nicholas is not well and will be taking early retirement at the end of the year. He thinks that is still a secret by the way, so be careful what you say. We had a meeting, he and I – well it was more of a clash really – anyway, I told him that I wanted to name the new Medical Annex after him. He objected. So I said I'd cut the funding to his carrot farm and he finally saw the light and agreed. So it is settled, the inauguration of the Nicholas Corbel Medical Centre with take place, *deo volente*, on December16th. Okay? So far so good. Now we come to the hard bit. I want to make the occasion truly memorable, historically. He deserves no less. Here is what I propose..."

The meeting continued for another two hours with many questions and a lot of laughter, but at the end, Siri called for a vote. After some hesitation all hands were raised in support.

"Not a word to anyone," she said as the meeting dissolved. "I will keep you individually informed of progress."

The people departed leaving only Siri and a tall, slim man with a carefully shaved head. His poise and physique could be that of a ballet dancer: Meet Isaac, leader of the skimmers.

"It is a bold plan, Miss McMillan. I like it. According to the schedule, the skimmers work will be finished and tested a week before the inauguration. We shall thus be available to help in any way."

"I'll remember that" said Siri.

## November 18th

Something was going on. Corbel could sense it. Everyone was so friendly. His paper in Berlin had been well received and there was some muttering about a Nobel Prize, but this he ignored.

In truth, he had begun the slow process of with-drawing, of handing over to younger researchers. He was tired too, and the cough...

For relaxation, Corbel took to sitting in the Clarke Alcove, from which he could watch the Skimmers at work. Guided by Isaac, they had built a grid, an icosahedron which, once charged, allowed them to skim, magnetically attached, to any corner and change web-lines at will.

He watched as they darted about, graceful as swallows, working in teams, guiding and connecting the pre-formed sections of the medical annex. The speed at which they worked astonished him. On the intercom we could listen to their chatter as they called to one another, and sang occasionally in their own private technical language. Each skimmer had a personal skim-name such as Albert, or Marie, or Rachel or Erwin: names given to them when they graduated. No two were alike. All were honourable.

By early December, all parts of the annex were wired, sealed and connected, The Skimmers began to work inside. The lights came on, and the gleaming new annex came to life.

## Dec 14th. Two days before the Inauguration.

Corbel had become pensive of late and was grateful for the solitude the Clarke alcove provided. He was remembering the early days of ISS, contemplating how big it had become when compared with the cramped place he had known when he started his laboratory there. And there, tethered not too far away, was the bulk of the great ship that was being built and would one day carry men and women to Mars.

Looking out, Corbel saw something that seemed strange. A slow-lift cargo bus had arrived at the airlock leading into the gleaming white Medical annex. A team of skimmers were clustered round obscuring his view. The air-lock door opened briefly and Corbel thought he saw something carried inside. More equipment he supposed, and thought no more about it.

## Dec 16th. Inauguration Day

A worldwide broadcast is planned.

Personally, Corbel thinks this is going too far, but no one seems to be listening to him anymore.

Siri has arrived at the ISS and has changed into a red dress which clashes with the colour of her hair, or so Nicholas thinks. Siri seems nervous too, more than he expected. And, of course, there are cameras poking their noses in everywhere.

## Inauguration (14.00 GMT)

The programme manager called for silence. "Going world wide and counting. 5. 4. 3. 2. 1. LIVE.

Around the world. Wherever international television could be screened, Siri's cheerful face appeared.

"Hello World. This programme is coming to you live from the International Space Station currently over the Pacific Ocean. It is a special day for us. Not only do we bid farewell to our friend, Professor Sir Nicholas Corbel, but we also celebrate the opening of a new medical installation and perhaps a new chapter of our journey into space. But first, allow me to introduce Professor Corbel."

All cameras turned on Nicholas. He had prepared a little speech, and was about to speak when an alarm bell rang. Siri turned, listening to her small headset, and then said. "I am sorry to interrupt you, Nick, but we are crossing live to an event..."

Immediately the image changes to show the inside of the Medical Annex. A doctor and two nurses can be seen.

Lying on a bed, but discretely covered, is a woman, clearly in the late stages of labour. It is a swift birth. One loud cry from the mother and the baby emerges head first into the world. The afterbirth is cleared discretely. No fuss. The camera focuses on the damp but smiling, brown-skinned face of the new mother. Moments later, the baby – a little girl – now wrapped in clean towels lies tucked in beside her mother. Her little face topped with a frizz of dark hair, peeps out, staring for a moment directly into the camera. And was that the hint of a smile? But then she yawns, and her eyes close. The doctor switched off the camera.

## 14.10

The image that appears on the screen after a few seconds is of Siri. She is kneeling on the ground and she is crying. Beside her is Nicholas, his arm round her shoulders. We can see that he too has tears. He whispers something in her ear. She smiles and nods and squeezes his hand. So...

While the attention of the world is thus engaged, strange things are happening in space.

On the dark side of the Moon, plumes of moon-dust erupt from many small craters, and then... unbelievable... a grey shape, circular it seems, slides up from the surface spilling clouds of dust from its dome.

On Earth, a cigar-shape, a mile long, rises from the depths of the ocean, breaks surface and lifts swiftly, unseen and silent.

High above, at a balancing point between Earth and Moon, lights suddenly blaze forth revealing an enormous shape, glittering like diamonds in sunlight. Everyone can see it.

Silently, the three ships glide into position, and hold still.

They are awaiting an invitation to join.

# Before They Left

## Colin Greenland

Ms Finn was telling Year Two about volcanoes. She showed them one in Hawaii. It was a mountain with fire coming out of it. The fire was full of rocks. The rocks were so hot they were burning.

Ms Finn told them the name of the volcano. It was a Hawaiian name. Clarity Ingram had stopped listening. She was staring at the volcano.

Ms Finn said it was very big, but there was another one a hundred times bigger. She said, "Can anyone guess where that is?"

Some children guessed America, Australia. Evie Winton guessed the North Pole. Clarity didn't guess anywhere. Then Ms Finn said the enormous volcano wasn't anywhere on Earth at all. It was on Mars.

After school, when Daddy came to pick her up, Clarity asked him. "Daddy?"

"What, princess?"

"Can we go to Mars?"

"Go where, princess?"

"Mars, Daddy."

"Mars? I don't expect so."

"Why not?"

"We're all right here. Aren't we? What would you like for tea?"

Later, in bed, Clarity told Monkey about the enormous volcano on Mars. Monkey grinned at her the way he always did. He didn't say anything. Once upon a time Monkey would have said *That's great, Clarity! Let's go and see it!* These days, Monkey didn't say as much as he used to. He didn't say anything at all, really. These days when you sat him up he tended to flop over in the middle, and the fur was coming off the top of his head.

When she woke up, the first thing Clarity thought about was pancakes with strawberry syrup. The next thing was the enormous volcano.

At break, Ms Finn was on playground duty. Clarity told her: "I want to go to Mars."

Ms Finn said, "Mars, Clarity? Why do you want to go to Mars?"

"I want to see the enormous volcano."

Ms Finn seemed pleased, the way she did when you remembered something she'd told you. "Well, Clarity," she said, "if you *can* do that, you'll be the first. The first Earth person, anyway. Think of that!"

By now there were other children pressing around them. They wanted to talk to Ms Finn too. Caleb was crying. He said Ajay had punched him. Teagen was holding one of her shoes.

Ms Finn smiled at them all. "Clarity's going to be the first Earth person on Mars."

Evie Winton was there. Wherever Clarity went, Evie always went too. She took hold of Clarity's hand. She was twiddling her hair, sucking it. "Are you really going to Mars, Clarity?"

"I expect so," Clarity said. "But I'm not going right this minute."

Evie looked happier. "Come and play then," she said.

The next person Clarity told was Kennedy, her big sister. "Kennedy," she said. "I'm going to Mars."

Kennedy was taking clothes out of a drawer and pulling faces at them. They were her clothes, but she didn't look as if she liked them.

"I'm going to see the enormous volcano," Clarity told her.

When Kennedy didn't answer, Clarity went right up behind her. "Kennedy, I'm going to *Mars*," she said again.

"I don't think you are, Clar," said Kennedy.

"You went to the Moon," Clarity pointed out.

Kennedy pulled another face. "That was a school trip."

Evie Winton's big brother Ollie was in Kennedy's class. Ollie had been on the trip too. Evie said that Ollie said that Kennedy was sick in the rocket.

Clarity played with a piece of her sister's hair, curling and uncurling it against her back. "Do they have volcanoes?"

Kennedy jerked her hair free. "*I* don't know."

She looked as if she was going to hit Clarity but then she stroked her cheek instead.

"The Moon's boring, sweetie," she said. "It's just rocks." She started pushing her clothes back into the drawer, getting them all screwed up and lumpy. "There isn't any air. You can't even go outdoors."

"I can go to Mars if I want to," Clarity said.

"Only if they send you."

"Who?"

"Duh. The Overlords."

Clarity knew about the Overlords. Everyone knew about the Overlords. They were as tall as trees and as black as coal. They had wings and long tails like fat black snakes.

"Did they send you to the Moon?"

"It's their rocket. We haven't got any rockets." Kennedy pushed the drawer. It wouldn't shut properly. Things were sticking out of it.

"It was Overlord Maltharika, Clarity," Kennedy said, as if Clarity had said something, as if she were being stupid. "You know Overlord Maltharika. He's the one who comes to school sometimes."

Clarity remembered Overlord Maltharika. He had spiky horns sticking out of his forehead and too many fingers on his hands. He was so big he had to crouch down to get through the door.

At school Evie Winton kept telling everyone Clarity Ingram was going to Mars. Clarity just smiled and held her nose up and walked away as if she had a secret.

In fact, when she thought about Overlord Maltharika, Clarity was less sure about Mars. Overlord Maltharika was like a giant black beetle.

In the summer they took Grandma and Grandpa to Sapmi and saw reindeer. Grandpa asked Clarity if she thought they were Father Christmas' reindeer, but they weren't flying, just shoving one another in among the trees and eating grass, like cows.

There were mountains. Clarity kept looking down to see if any were volcanoes, but if they were she didn't spot them. There was no fire, only snow.

Then school started again. One day at break a tall car came.

Men in black leather suits got out and stood around it. The next to get out was an Overlord.

The Overlord looked as if he were wearing black leather too, though really that was just their skin. He had a big thick belt around his middle with machines on it, with lights on them flickering. When he stood up straight his men only came up to his waist.

Some of the children went on playing. Some stood staring, the little ones clinging to the fence. Some of the older children went closer. Evie called Clarity back. Clarity ignored her. She went closer too.

The Overlord stretched his shoulders. His wings flared wide, then settled again.

One of his men was speaking to a boy in Year Eight. "Tell Mrs Dutt Overlord Maltharika has arrived."

Clarity slipped between the Overlord's men. She got so close she could nearly touch him. His legs were like shiny black trees, right in front of her, the things on his belt hanging down like metal fruit. It hurt her neck to look up at him.

"I want to go to Mars," she said.

She said it as loudly as she could. It didn't sound very loud. Behind her was the noise of everyone playing, shouting, laughing.

But the Overlord had heard her. He leaned his face down to inspect her. He had big sunglasses on. The sunglasses were as black as his face. She could smell him. He smelled like pineapple.

"Clarity Ingram," said the Overlord.

His voice was very deep and soft, like a big metal ball rolling somewhere under the ground. Clarity's heart jumped when he said her name, but she wasn't shocked. The Overlords know *everything*.

One of the men was talking to her. He had a beard, and there was a wire coming out of his ear. Clarity ignored him. "I want to go to Mars," she told the Overlord again.

One of the things on the Overlord's belt was a fat sort of bottle. He pulled a tube out of it now and put the end of it to his cheek, where the holes were. There was a wet hissing noise, as if he were squirting something out of the bottle into his face.

"Why do you want to go to Mars, Clarity Ingram?" said Overlord Maltharika.

"I want to see the enormous volcano."

The Overlord flicked a finger at one of the men: not the one with the beard, one of the others. The Overlord said a word to him. The man looked at his phone, then said something back. Clarity couldn't understand what they said.

"Olympus Mons," the Overlord said then, to Clarity.

Clarity didn't understand that either. In the giant sunglasses she saw the playground reflected: two playgrounds full of two lots of children, all curved around like the backs of spoons.

"No," said the Overlord.

Clarity felt she was going to cry. She shouted at him. "*Why not?*"

She felt the fingers of the man with the beard, grasping her shoulder. The Overlord hadn't moved. He was like a big statue looking down at her.

Clarity was very frightened suddenly. Then she saw the Overlord straightening up, rising away from her, very fast, his head and shoulders shooting up into the sky.

The man with the beard lifted Clarity so her feet were almost off the ground. He swept her up the drive towards the door, where some of the teachers were. She saw them coming to get her, hurrying to take her away from him.

In class, Ms Finn talked about the Overlords, and all the good things they give us, and how important it is to be polite to them. Evie kept looking at Clarity with big round eyes and sucking the ends of her hair.

At the end of the day, when she came to collect Clarity, Mummy said Mrs Dutt wanted to see her.

Clarity waited outside in the corridor. Children stood at the end of the corridor and looked at her.

Mummy wasn't in there very long. When she came out, she looked puzzled. She sat down beside Clarity.

"This is for you," she said, "apparently."

She gave Clarity a piece of paper. The paper was folded in half. Clarity opened it. At the top, in capital letters, was printed:

FROM THE OFFICE OF OVERLORD MALTHARIKA.

Under that were five words, written with an ordinary pen. Clarity thought one of the Overlord's men must have written them for him, because the Overlords' fingers were too big, and there were too many of them.

The words said:

*Because you're going somewhere better.*

Clarity forgot about Mars after that, and the enormous volcano. The sun went on shining, and there was a tree at the end of the garden that she wanted to climb. It was too hard at first, harder than she'd thought. Kennedy wasn't interested, but Daddy helped, and in a while she was sitting up on a branch, one leg either side, riding it like a horse.

It wasn't many weeks later that she had the dream.

In the dream, Clarity was in a wood. Evie was there, and Teagen. Everybody was, all the children, even Ajay. In the dream they were dancing, all of them together, under a full moon. When they danced, Clarity thought the trees would be in their way, but then they weren't. In the dream she heard a voice saying *Let's move the trees.* It was a girl's voice, but she didn't know whose.

It wasn't Kennedy. Kennedy wasn't there. Kennedy was somewhere else, with Mummy and Daddy and all the grown-ups. They didn't need grown-ups any more. They just had to want the trees to move, all of them together, wanting it; and the trees moved. If they wanted it, the Moon would move.

In her sleep, Clarity laughed. It was easy.

Then the dream changed. There was no one there, not even Clarity. There was just Maltharika, the Overlord. You couldn't see his face, just his back. He was looking up at the sky.

The thing about the Overlords was, even when you could see their faces, you couldn't tell what they were feeling; but in the dream Clarity knew Overlord Maltharika was sad.

In the dream, at the very edge of dreaming, she heard his deep, rolling voice, speaking to her again, speaking to all of them. Saying *Goodbye.*

Clarity woke up then and saw Monkey grinning at her.

# Drawn from the Eye

## Jeff Noon

The guards at the interface station wouldn't allow her through. The face of Madison Glade, known and loved throughout the two worlds, was flagged up on a screen as a potential risk: *association with known undesirables.* She pleaded her case, demanded access, told them it must all be a mistake. The guards were programmed with two emotions and compassion wasn't one of them.

Maddie stood at the frontier. The lunar village shimmered in the portal, just beyond her reach.

The manager arrived, a pale-faced woman in a fitted two-piece suit. "Sadly, we can't make exceptions, even for well-known and popular entertainers such as yourself." It was the final word. But Maddie had already spied her parents waiting for her as promised in the lounge area: there they were on the other side of the wall of light. How old they looked, how frail. Her mother was very ill, soon to pass away. The thought was a trigger. Maddie started to run. She slipped between the two guards, jumped over a barrier and leapt full pelt into the shimmer wall. A siren screamed, voices called out in alarm. Ahead, her mother and father looked shocked, and then expectant. Their arms rose up in greeting. She was almost there! If she could only reach out a little further, their hands would surely touch...

The world slowed around her, almost to a standstill.

Maddie had never experienced hyperspace before. It was a strange feeling, a sense of time gathering in the channels of her flesh and holding her tight. From some infinite distance she remembered the news reports of the grand opening, the phrase used by the first citizen to take the journey: *It's like dancing with Einstein in treacle.* How true: a sluggish waltz around the distant rim of a clockface, waiting for the next second to click away.

Now she was being pulled back by a guard. Where moments

before her parents seemed but a few short steps away, now they appeared to her across the vastness of space. Too far, too far. Tears fell from her eyes only to coagulate on her skin and take off on their own journeys, two silver globules slowly drifting away. One of them made it through the portal, into lunar space. The other teardrop followed Maddie back to Earth.

The collector waited for his audience to respond to his story. He was old now and it took him longer each day to conduct the tour. He pointed to the nearest exhibit, to the twin specimens: caught and classified, carefully preserved, both held suspended in mid-air at the centre of their own force field, displayed in two identical glass cabinets, labelled and marked and measured and each given a score – seven out of ten (*Earth Teardrop*), and nine out of ten (*Lunar Teardrop*). The collector called it the most perfect example of celebrity sadness: a life turned liquid. "And more than fifty years ago now, can you imagine?" None of the museum's visitors could, it sounded like ancient history. "Can any of you even recall a single melody or lyric by Madison Glade? No, of course not! All that remains, ladies and gentlemen, are these two globules of mucin, lipids, lysozyme, lactoferrin, lipocalin, lacritin, immunoglobulins, glucose, sodium, and potassium." Now the visitors looked confused. "Lachrymal fluid." Still no response. "Teardrops." Sighing, the collector hurried the people on, stopping only at the Marilyn Monroe selection. "I am one of the few upon this world to understand the true nature of lachrymation. There are only twenty-seven of us in the guild." He laughed. "My collection has been gathered over many years, some of them purchased from traders, others I dare to admit stolen from rivals." Another laugh. "Many more were taken directly from the eyes and cheeks of lovers, friends, enemies, strangers, from people both ordinary and famous, from those who cry easily and from those whose tears have to be pried out of them using a series of special instruments. We call this the *gleaning* of tears." He revelled in the sound of the word. "Gleaning!" But he was losing them now. One of the younger kids reached out to disturb the Elvis Presley exhibit. He shooed the little blighter away from the stand and ushered them all towards the exit door.

"Thank you, thank you for visiting with us today. Goodbye. Please tell your friends."

The collector slept badly that night and woke early before the dawn. He took a seat at his office desk and contemplated his few belongings. Almost all of his earnings had been spent on the museum and its contents. It was getting harder every day: attendances were dwindling, funds were running out. And he was getting tired, tired of the effort required. He stood up and walked over to the display cabinet on the far side of the room. Here his rarest examples were kept, safely under lock and key. They glistened within their separate jars: five translucent beads, each one carefully preserved. The jars were labelled with the shedder's name and the date of release.

He remembered as a child watching a moth drink tears from the eyes of a docile sheep. This was the beginning of his fascination. The first tear he ever collected was drawn from the sallow cheek of his mother as she lay on her sickbed. He hardly knew what he was doing that day, his young hands trembling as they went about their task. He lost four of her tears before at last managing to capture a single specimen in the bowl of a teaspoon. Passion took over. As he grew older, the collector travelled along many strange and sometimes hazardous roads, seeking out exceptional items, and at every turn he'd kept to the guild's code of silence regarding the teardrop and its secret potential.

But now death was closing in. It was time to reveal the truth.

He went back to his work desk and started to write in his journal. His rivals and colleagues would curse me for this, and deny all knowledge of the secret. "Let them curse," he said to himself. "Let them damn my name." Night was fading into day and soon conditions would be ideal for his final experiment.

He continued to write.

*The mind treats raw experience as a series of shocks that it must quickly assess in case of any physical or psychological danger that might be present. Overwhelmingly unpleasant incidents or feelings will be pushed into the deepest core of the subconscious, to lie there forgotten unless some further stimulus rouses them once more. There is, however, one further layer of forgetting, and that is to reject the memory completely, to rid the psyche entirely of the source of the pain or the sadness. Teardrops are nothing more or less than the vessels within which such terrible memories travel as they leave the body, seeping away into the world, there to be lost, to be wiped clean by a handkerchief or a fingertip. To fall on the page of a book, or a letter from a loved one. To evaporate.*

*Such is the true and fragile nature of the tear. And yet between the shedding and the demise, various delicate instruments – a suction bubble for instance, or an electrostatic loop – can be employed to catch the tear. It can be preserved over time, it can be fixed in place and a special light shone through it, enabling the sadness within to be viewed on a screen. By these methods I have witnessed the emotions of others. I would close my eyes after seeing these visions of despair, and then force them open to watch some more, addicted as I was, as I still am, to such melancholic pleasures. It is a pleasure tinged with its own peculiar sorrow, because the very act of viewing destroys the tear. Which is best, to experience the exquisite beauty of melancholy and by experiencing it destroy it, or not to view sadness at all? Such is the dilemma all in the guild must confront. Perhaps it is this constant battle between restraint and release that means that we who have viewed the intimate secret of the tears rarely cry on our own account...*

The sun was coming up. It was time. The collector extinguished the lamps and pulled the curtains tightly across the windows. The room was dark. Only a single slit remained, in the wall directly facing the sunrise. The light rays crept onward. He took a jar from the cabinet and freed its contents from the preserving medium. Carefully, his hands still and sure despite his age and despite the magnitude of the undertaking, he placed the glistening droplet in the viewing frame. A beam of sunlight shone through the wall slit. Through a series of five different concave mirrors, the beam was focused precisely upon the droplet. The light struck. A teardrop exploded. Colours flared outward in a rainbow's arc, bathing the wall screen in a mist of light. There was no other word for it; a *mist* of light. Now the beam faded as the sun moved on, leaving the room once more in darkness. The collector walked over to the screen, switching on the red-shaded lamp that he kept there. He saw that the mist had become fixed to the screen. Slowly it melted into a soft focus, the flecks of colour forming a hazy image. Tiny details could be made out at first, and then areas of clearer shape. He moved closer to the screen, knowing he had a few seconds only before the image disappeared. He brought to mind the moment of gleaning, when he'd followed Madison Glade through the lunar portal, the next in line that day. He'd already caught and preserved the Earth droplet, and once through the shimmer he'd moved quickly to catch the lunar teardrop before it broke up. Such skill he'd had in his youth! But his real prize remained the teardrop he'd told no one about, not even his learned colleagues in the guild.

The third teardrop. His most beautiful possession.

The one he'd seen in the shimmer itself, held aloft in the slowed down world of hyperspace. This was the droplet he had now destroyed, in order to produce the mist on the screen. This was a tear shed in a realm between worlds, remaining there for a few moments before his collecting tools took charge. It contained mysteries, surely it did, the secrets of the universe. The collector stared at the mist and he saw within it a landscape, and a figure of some kind, a human figure. A woman. She moved and breathed and sighed. Within her body were the collected emotions of all who had passed through the lunar portal up to that point, and all who had passed through since, as time looped back upon itself continually: love, desire, hatred, despair, hope, and most of all sadness. The woman was bowed down, her heart heavy with the weight she carried.

The collector knew that these were his final moments of life. Yet even as he watched, the woman was already moving away, the vision fading.

And something happened then, something that hadn't happened to him in a very long time, not in years, not in decades. The gland above each eye, situated behind the eyelid, started to secrete a fluid. This fluid seeped through a pair of ducts, into the space between the eyeball and the lids. When he blinked the fluid was spread across the surface of the eye. It gathered in the lacrimal lake, it flowed via the puncta and through the canaliculi at the inner corner of the eyelids. It sparkled for a moment in the red light of the lamp and then tipped over the rim of flesh, skimming the lashes. Now the fluid travelled down his face, along the deep crevices age had cut there, until it reached his lips and he tasted salt.

The collector wept.

# Roads of Silver, Paths of Gold

## Emmi Itäranta

They brought the bones into the forest and buried them under the tree, and the bear's skull they hung on a high branch. The smooth eye sockets stared where their light rises.

They no longer sing the songs of old. They do not come in the middle of the bright-burnished day but at night, if they come at all. But I am still here: keeping watch, counting the moments until I must take to my path again.

There were only three of them this time.

The two younger ones would rather have been somewhere else. The oldest wanted to be alone. He wished to talk to me, or to what he thinks I am.

*Honeypaw, my woodland apple,*
*my curve-claw, my forest beauty,*
he chanted in his mind.

Ancient words, echoing across the language of his people from time before they bound their songs in books. Lights brushed the trees and the engine sound drew away as the bone-bringers left, but the hum still rippled through me.

*From the shoulders of the Great Bear,*
*from the branches of the tall tree,*
*along skies and cloud-strewn birdways,*
*paths of gold and roads of silver.*

I have known this chant as long as I can remember. Once, it reached all the way across the universe and woke me in my distant world. So I thought then.

We are all dust in space, emptiness until someone acknowledges the possibility of our existence.

My world was a world of silent plains and frozen seas, and those who shared it with me were silent too. They were content to gather around hot crevices in the seabed, to feed on what the water gave them and remain where they were. But I had a mind of a different persuasion. I would swim to the surface and look at the lights in the black sky, and I would dream of other worlds.

I still cannot explain what happened. At first, there was darkness. Then there was a hum that made a crack in the blackness. The strange music echoed in a distance so great that I could barely imagine it. It washed over me and receded again. At the time I was not familiar with the words, but behind them was a sentiment that took hold of me: a summons. It shaped the silence as I floated among ice and rested next to fire-hot underwater fountains.

I asked my dust-family if any of them could hear the music. Most of them did not. Those who did were not interested. But for me it grew louder by the moment. One night, when I was sky-watching, the darkness above unfolded. I took one last glance at my world, latched onto the hum and allowed it to carry me.

It pulled me out of the sea and silence. Lights and blackness flickered past. I travelled for a long time. Along birdways, from the shoulders of stars, along roads of silver and paths of gold I arrived into their world.

Perhaps my essence was so different here that this caused me to lose the hum, or else the journey had been too demanding. I was met with silence. I was frightened and sought a way back, but the heavens had closed.

I had no choice but to stay.

For a time I observed. I saw life take many shapes, all alien to me. The tall-growing creatures with green crowns and deep underground limbs shifted curiously when they sensed my presence. The brown-coated, red-coated, grey-coated things that walked on four legs, the flying things great and small, they would stare at me and sometimes come closer. But I was little more than specks of light; they soon lost interest. The creatures walking on two feet I found the strangest of all. The movements of their minds were complex, and they looked to powers invisible to them to find fortune.

Eventually one day I heard the hum again. I followed it into a village, into a small tent made from animal skins. The hum grew into a chant.

For the first time I saw the creature calling me.

Her face was light brown and lines like rifts in stone split it. She swung her long, grey hair from side to side as she chanted, and on her brow she wore a headdress with two antlers. Her eyes were closed.

When I entered the tent, she opened her eyes.

Then she kneeled in front of me, bowed her forehead to the ground, and offered me something in a bowl.

It was a glistening, red heart, large enough to be a human's.

I had already learned that few of them could see me or talk to me. When they did, they believed me to be something other than I was. They were limited by their human senses and by what they were able to conceive of in their hearts and minds. She, the first summoner, did see, but not how I would have seen myself, or how my faraway dust-family would have. Instead, she spoke to me as if I was something of her world. She called me forest-mistress and needle-fur. She would bring me presents: food and drink made from all things that grew. I had no material body in this world, no way to consume her offerings, but I came to recognise them as tokens of respect and gratitude.

Seasons had shifted once or twice, when I finally understood what I was in her mind. The people of her village attached long pieces of wood to their shoes and slid along snow to a hole in a rock. There they began to make noise. After a while, a creature with dark brown fur, sharp-edged paws and dangerous strength in its muscles emerged. It slashed the air with groggy claws, but the hunters surrounded it, their metal blades aimed at its soft flesh.

Blood ran wet and red as they drove their spears into the animal.

When the heart of the beast had stopped beating, they carried the body into their village, skinned it and cut off its head, singing songs that praised its beauty and strength. They brought it into a clean-swept house, placed the skin on the wall and the head in a steaming pot on the stove, and around a long table they drank and ate.

After, they took the bones to the forest and buried them under the tree which already held several white skulls on its branches. They hung the skull high, the eye sockets looking where their light rises.

They thanked the bear and the woodland spirits for the gift of meat and furs, and requested that the forest take the bones back so it could give them new bears.

The first summoner spoke to me then. *Hongatar*, she called me. She looked at the space-dust of me and, where the others saw nothing, she saw the mother spirit of all bears, who had brought them into the world from beyond the stars.

They gave me gifts and spoke to me. The first summoner stopped dancing and breathing and turned to dust. After her came a second and third and many more, for their lives were brittle. I learned to listen to their messages and understand their words. In exchange for the gifts, they asked for protection, for good crops and healthy children and fish in their lakes. The more they spoke to me, the stronger I grew. To thank them, I tried to provide them with what I could. I whispered to fish under the waves so they would swim nearer the village. I sighed softly in the ears of cows on pastures, so they would find their way to the greenest grass. I sang to oats in the fields, so they would grow tall and golden. When the enemy threatened the village, I raised a storm on the lake and filled the sky with fire, so the strange ships could not come ashore.

Sometimes a summoner would set their spirit free from the chains of their body. That was when I was most easily able to commune with them. They would ask for advice and request my protection in healing the sick. I sought my memory for the knowledge of my faraway family, and the sick would heal. I took summoners on distant journeys, along roads of silver and paths of gold, through holes in space to other places. They drew maps of them on animal skins stretched over wooden frames, so they could beat a rhythm to hasten the journey and find their way back.

I was no longer dust in space. I belonged.

But somewhere along the way, things shifted. They felled the trees and tore down the skulls and stopped singing to me. They changed the winds and waters, put their poisons in them. Summoners are fewer now. Those who bring the bones to the forest are also few. They have not stopped taking, but they have stopped giving back.

The trees are weak. The animals are weak. The faith of humans in anything beyond themselves is weak.

I am weak. Once fire and thunder, I am now specks of light and dust, my voice worn to a whisper.

I have found myself star-gazing, looking for the path along which I came, a long time ago. If I do find it and make my way home, I do not know what awaits me there. Will my dust-family have become something else, so that I will be alien to them and they will cast me out, or worse? Will they be the same, but I so different we can no longer speak to each other? Or will a story have survived among them of a curious, foolish creature who many ages ago listened to the hum of other worlds and left, never to be seen again?

During flowaway seasons when light waxes and wanes, I wonder if the chant of the first summoners did more than bring me into this world. I remember nothing clearly before waking up to it. Is this because it was my moment to wake up then, and it coincided with the music from the stars?

Or is it because that music brought me to being?

We are all dust in space, emptiness until someone acknowledges the possibility of our existence.

Back when I was strong, humans believed in what I was in their minds. My power faded with their faith, as the power of winds and water and animals waned once people stopped understanding they were part of the shifting seasons, rather than separate from them.

Yet there is another possibility. It has held me to this world since I began dreaming of returning to my home that is home no more.

Maybe they did not bring me to being.

Maybe I brought them.

Maybe their chant was born the moment I woke up and was able to imagine such a thing. Maybe, until then, their world was a mere possibility among others, and being acknowledged by a living creature, no matter how far away, turned that possibility into sand and seas and skies, and trees and animals and humans.

I do not know what will happen to them when I leave.

Not long ago I picked up a faint hum, a wordless sentiment that washed over me and receded again. It is so distant I can barely sense it. There is little time before my strength wears away altogether.

One of these brief days, as their planet circles the sun, the darkness above will unfold and I will travel again. I will take to birdways and shoulders of stars, to roads of silver and paths of gold. I will follow the music of the other world that may only have just been born.

As I go, I will imagine a tall tree, and on its branches a flame-white skull. The sheen of the rising light burnishes the smooth eye sockets that no longer see how everything turns to dust.

*Translation note:*

*Honeypaw, woodland apple, curve-claw and forest beauty are terms borrowed from Runo 46 in George C. Schoolfield (ed.),* **The Kalevala: Epic of the Finnish People** *(Helsinki, Finland: Otava, 1988). Translation by Eino Friberg.*

# The Fugue

## Stephanie Holman

Giea looked up, blinking in the sunlight. She was sitting in a warm, bright conservatory, she was knitting, and there was a man sitting opposite her. The chair she sat on seemed to be moulded to her, with barely any filler left in the seat cushion. The man coughed and turned a page of his book. He was old. He looked worn through, his hair and skin were faded; brittle in his own clothing.

Giea looked down at her own hands and was shocked by the crumpled skin and raised veins. She put the knitting down gently. The man looked up at her small movement.

"You all right, Gina?" He grinned at her.

She smiled automatically, then nodded. "Tea time. I've just not moved in a bit." As if on cue her back seized and only responded with small shooting pains. Giea shuffled forward in her seat and levered her body up by holding onto the chair arms. The man watched her slow progress.

The conservatory was off the kitchen, so she didn't have to shuffle far before finding the kettle. She filled it to the maximum, so it would take longer to boil. The man's reflection in the conservatory's glass door had gone back to reading his book. Giea did not run to the bathroom. She calmly padded down the hallway, and only when she had locked the bathroom door did she breathe again. She turned on the overhead light and looked into the mirror. She was as old as the man. The unforgiving light showed her to be as faded as him; pure white hair and beige clothes hung off her skinny frame. She touched the mirror, and then her own face. She did not recognise the face.

She sniffed back tears. She tapped the left-hand corner of the mirror twice. After a moment, the mirror lit up like a computer monitor, and light spiralled at its centre before it leapt from the glass and an image of a startled young Crepit stood before her. It stared back at Giea.

"Confirm secure line." Giea stuttered.

The Crepit's scales shimmered and the light from the mirror spread around them both; encapsulating them in a bubble with the mirror.

"Line secured. What're you?" The Crepit peered at Giea.

"Agent 24-7635. Report." Giea barked back.

"Hold." It closed its eye for a moment, "There is no record of that agent number."

"Get me, Hage!" Giea roared, "Get me, Hage, now!"

The mirror went black and the Crepit disappeared. Giea held her breath until the light returned.

The image was of Hage. He was older too. He gasped at Giea and reached his limbs towards her.

"What happened?" She croaked at him, his shock did not make her feel any better.

"Giea? Is it really you?" he whispered.

"Of course, it's me. Why didn't my agent code work?"

"You've been gone – "

"I can see that!" She roared again, "I can see by this face that I've been gone! What happened, why wasn't I pulled out?"

"You never signed in. You never contacted us, we thought you'd gone native –" Hage spluttered.

Giea half laughed, "You thought I wanted to stay here?"

"You demanded the expedition," Hage argued.

"I'm the best qualified to watch this race. Best to blend in." She paused, then whispered, "I don't understand, why didn't you come to find me?"

"We did. You turned away every agent we sent for you."

"What are you talking about? I never –"

"Giea, you sent me away!" Hage rushed her and his image pixelated as it struck her flesh. "I altered myself for you, I came to you, I begged you to leave with me. You acted as if I were mad, like you didn't know me. You sent me away." He shuddered a heavy breath.

"I didn't. I don't," Giea shook her head, "I don't remember anything."

"What's the last thing you do remember?" Hage pressed on.

"The test." Giea brightened with the memory, "The mirror connection being tested. It all seemed fine. Then I got ready, and I went out that night. I was due to meet with –"

"The mark. Peter?" Hage prompted.

"He's out there now." Giea looked down at her spotted hands. There was a ring on her left hand. "I'm married."

Hage scales rippled, "Hold still."

"What?" Giea jumped as a blue light appeared and ran over her body. "What are you doing?" She demanded.

"You're 82 Earth years old Giea." Hage stopped for a moment and then breathed out, "You've had children."

Giea moaned and ran her hands over her deformed body.

"They'll all have to be destroyed," Hage muttered, not looking at her.

Giea turned cold eyes on to Hage. "It's not their fault."

"How did you even have children? Didn't their hospitals check your blood?" Hage didn't seem to expect an answer.

"I don't know," Giea said.

"How far did they take things in the surgery to make you seem human?"

"I don't know." She spoke through gritted teeth.

"I'll check…" Hage finally looked at her. "I'm sorry, I know you're scared."

"How do you know what I am?" Giea wailed, "I don't even know what I'm feeling, so don't throw your guilt at me. Just get me out of here."

Hage looked startled, "I can't do that."

"What are you talking about? Send down the transport."

"The transports not there anymore."

"What? Why not?" Giea demanded.

"We got all the information we needed on that race years ago. And you were for all intents and purposes gone." Hage shrugged at her.

"I'm right here," she screamed at Hage. "I'm right here! Send them back for me."

Hage was just shaking his head, "I'll need to speak with the authorities. This is unprecedented."

"Hage, you come back for me," Giea finally cried, and reached for the image of her friend. "Come back for me, please don't leave me here."

"Stay there, I'll speak to you as soon as I can."

"I can't stay in here much longer, he's out there. He'll want to know what's going on."

"You've managed him all this time. Just keep being Gina for a little longer." Hage took one last look at her. "I'm so sorry." Then he was gone.

The light containing their conversation dimmed and finally winked off. Giea held her hand over her mouth to stifle her own moans. She splashed her face with cold water and got her breathing under control. When she opened the bathroom door, Peter was waiting outside. She gasped and pretended to laugh.

"Silly, you startled me." He let her push past him back to the kitchen.

"You were in there long enough. Feeling all right?" Peter shadowed her footsteps.

"Yes. Just a bit stiff from sitting around." She busied herself with their tea and jumped as Peter patted her shoulder.

"What's wrong, someone walk over your grave?" Peter laughed and took the tea she handed him. He went back to the conservatory. She realised she had made him a weak tea with two sugars. Muscle memory to her rescue.

She called out to him, "I'm going to lie down for a bit. Back's giving me jip."

"Yep, I'll wake you if you snore." Peter chuckled.

Giea made her way back to the hallway. On the walls were pictures. Weddings, christenings, school plays, proms, more weddings. Grandchildren. She stumbled as she took in an entire life, her own life. It was all there. All her lies. Did she really choose this? She choked on tears and hurried to her room. She could remember the faces of her children. Her beautiful girls. She could remember how to make a stupid cup of tea but she had no idea why she had stayed on this planet.

Her room was overly floral and there was a pile of murder mystery books by a single bed. She lay outstretched on the bed, and her back immediately eased. If only her mind could be as easily quietened. Hage would come for her, or he would try. But if he did, would it be for her, or to kill her children? She couldn't let him. She had done this. She had stayed on a tiny planet, married an alien man and bore his children. She got up and looked through her room. Spare reading glasses and an address book on the bedside table. No notes in the books on the shelves. An old brown leather case in her wardrobe held only musty property papers. A jewellery box in her knicker drawer held fake diamonds and shell necklaces. Nothing to show who she really was. Giea, the Crepit disguised as Gina, the human.

Giea made her way back downstairs, back to the bathroom. She waited for a few minutes by the mirror but Hage did not reappear. Deflated, she went back to the kitchen, where Peter was sitting at the breakfast bar, reading a newspaper.

"Feeling better?" He didn't look up from the paper.

"Yeah, only takes a few minutes of stretching out for the back to feel normal again." She wanted to get to the garden, to the fresh air. Peter grabbed her arm as she passed him, "Did you reach Hage this time?"

"What are you talking about?" Giea stammered.

"I thought you were over this." He dropped her arm and got down from his stool. He huffed at her, "After all these years, I thought you were better."

"What're you talking about?" Giea stalled, trying to think.

"Come on, Gina, you think this is the first time you've woken up?" Peter ran hands over his skull, obviously agitated.

"Woken up?" Giea backed away from him, trying to get back to the bathroom. Her head spun in pain and she wanted to put a door between her and Peter.

Peter sighed. "From the fugue. Thinking you're Giea, the Crepit."

She gasped. "How'd you know that word?"

Peter gave a sad laugh. "Because you told me."

Giea's head pounded but she kept backing away from him. "Peter, please, you're scaring me."

"You're in the fugue, Gina. I thought if I let you reach the mirror this time, if you finally realised this was all in your mind, it might be over."

"I don't know what you're on about?" Giea begged.

"You've always had these funny moments. The first night we met you had some sort of turn. The doctors called it a fugue. I've not left your side since then." Giea's vision started to blur and she caught herself on the kitchen side.

"Why are you doing this?" Giea held a hand out at him to keep him back. "Who are you really, why are you keeping me here?"

"Because you asked me to." Peter just nodded at the shock on her face. "Come on Gina, love, try to remember, you wanted to stay here with me."

Giea crumpled to the kitchen floor. He was keeping her here, but how? She felt sick with the pain in her head. She had told the truth, somehow; they had made her tell the truth and they hadn't believed her. Something must have gone wrong with the surgery to look human. Peter knelt before her and she whimpered as he reached for her.

He whispered, "The doctors wanted you to stay at the hospital. But you wanted to stay here with me. And sometimes you think of another life, this incredible story you created. But you love me. You always come back to me. You'll remember your real life soon." Taking an EpiPen from his cardigan pocket, Peter injected her.

Giea thought of Hage, "They'll kill our girls," she hissed at Peter, as the pain increased and she fainted. Peter caught her head and gently laid her down on the floor.

"No, they won't. It'll all be better when you wake up. You always are. It's just another one your funny turns." Peter stroked his wife's finely crafted alien head, "It'll be alright love, I'll never let you forget me."

# Memories of a Table

## Chris Beckett

'So, is that everyone? Excellent. I'm Jodi and I'll be your guide this morning. Welcome to the New York City Museum of Chronotronic Archaeology. What you're about to see are fragments of past events, the oldest going back millions of years. Some people call them reconstructions, but we don't go along with that. A Roman vase dug up out of the ground is still the original vase, even if it's been broken and glued together without its handles, isn't it? Well, it's exactly the same with what you're about to experience here. All of the past events you're going to see are fragments, but they're not copies. They're the events themselves, playing out in front of your eyes.'

It's an unusual-looking museum, essentially a corridor, lined on both sides with a dozen doors. Jodi the guide has been standing in front of one of these doors and now she opens it, gesturing to the rest of us to enter. There are about twenty in the group and, with one exception, everyone has a friend with them, or a partner, or relative; the exception being me. We hesitate. No one really wants to be first to go through, but a no-nonsense African American woman in her thirties steps forward, towing her reluctant partner after her. There are yelps of surprise and delight from within, and the rest of us follow.

A pine forest surrounds us. We can see it, we can hear the wind blowing through the leaves, we can smell the resin. Jodi points out an enormous dragonfly alighting on a tree trunk, its wings trembling. It rubs its mouthparts with its forelimbs, crawls a few inches up the trunk. There's a screeching noise from some way off in the forest. The dragonfly pauses, rubs its mouthparts once more, and

And then nothing. We're all standing in complete darkness. Jodi flips on the lights with a remote she carries in her hand.

'That was collected in Antarctica,' she says. 'It's taking place seventy million years ago in the Cretaceous era, and it lasts all of nine seconds, which is not a lot, but is more than four times longer than any other specimen of that age in any museum anywhere in the world.'

'Was that a dinosaur screeching?' asks a ten-year-old boy.

'It could very well be. We just don't know.'

'Sounded like it was some way off to the right,' a middle-aged Indian man says. 'Could you not go back to Antarctica and see what else can be found in that general direction?'

'I'm afraid it doesn't work like that. The chronotronic record starts to degrade from day one and, when you go back as far as the Cretaceous, you're dealing with objects that may have been broken, scattered, lumped together with other objects of different ages, and broken and scattered again. It's much like fossils, I guess. You find a whole one here and there, but that's the exception rather than the rule. Right. Let's have a look at something else.'

Jodi leads us a few yards down the corridor before opening another door. We are instantly hit by a blast of oppressive heat and blinding light. Suddenly a human voice – it seems to come from the sun itself – cries out in pain from somewhere above us. And then abruptly it all vanishes – cry, light, heat – all at the same moment.

'It makes me angry every time,' says Jodi as she turns on the lights. 'This was a truly unique and irreplaceable specimen which has been irreparably damaged, not by the passing of time but by sheer human stupidity. Anyhow, does anyone want to guess where that event is taking place?'

'Somewhere hot!' calls out a red haired woman, with a big, satisfied grin, as if she thought she was being remarkably observant.

'That's for sure! In fact this specimen was collected from a small piece of stone that was purchased in Jerusalem sometime in the eighteenth century by a young aristocrat on the Grand Tour. Only a few years ago, his great great great great grandson, the stone's current owner, was persuaded by one of these so-called free-lancers to let him carry out a chronotronic analysis on it to see if the claims made for it could be substantiated. This should have been a relatively simple task, but somehow or other the wretched man managed to destroy that stone's entire chronotronic record from the relevant period, apart from that tiny fragment you've just experienced.'

'So what claims *were* made for it?' asks a young Chinese man in a baseball cap.

'Oh, did I not say? The stone was sold to that young aristocrat with the assurance that it had lain at the foot at the True Cross. You *may* just have been present at the Crucifixion, but now we'll never know. How maddening is that? But come on, people, let's go and look at something else.'

The twenty-one people, in their twos and threes and fours, file out of the room. I am the last. Jodi gives me a little smile as I go past. It's not an unfriendly smile, but I feel the sad old loner is being sized up, and not being given a particularly high score. And then she frowns slightly, as if it's struck her that she's seen me before but she can't quite remember where.

'Oh yes, Jodi,' I mutter under my breath as I emerge into the corridor, 'you've seen me before all right!'

The next room contains ten whole minutes from seventeenth century Boston. Everyone starts getting a bit restive after the first five. It's just a bit of street, after all, with people passing from time to time. Once we've got used to the funny outfits, it just isn't that interesting any more. Amazing really! Here we are, standing in a street in the reign of King James the First and we're bored.

Or, in my case, desperate to get on to what really brought me here.

Sensing the general feeling, Jodi leads us out of the room while the events, such as they are, continue to unfold.

'History books and movies have led us to think of the past as a series of exciting events,' she observes a little tartly, 'but what chronotronics teaches us is that life isn't really about the big dramas. That stone from Jerusalem may possibly be an exception, but even there, who knows, that cry may well just be a roofer who hit his thumb with a hammer. Okay, now here's a slice of life from the 1970s. The sample comes from an old bar table from England that someone picked up from a recycling centre. A pub table, as they'd call it over there. We think it's from the city of Bristol, but we haven't yet pinpointed the exact location. The particles extracted from the table have remained in an unusually stable configuration so

133

it's been possible to extract a fairly lengthy continuous sequence. I'll wait outside, and when you've had enough you can come and join me.'

So this is it. This is what I came all this way for. I'm trembling, my mouth is dry, my heart is pounding, but I'm trying not to show it. The pub table is right in front of us as we walk in. A young couple are sitting at it. Oh dear God! We can walk round them, look right into their faces. They've got no idea we're there.

They're both nineteen years old. He's got curly brown hair down to his shoulders and a very thin wispy beard. His face is pleasant and I suppose averagely good-looking, in a mild, unassertive sort of way. He's wearing jeans that flare out from the knee – loons, didn't we used to call them? – and a kind of long-sleeved T-shirt that does the same kind of thing from the elbow down. She is beautiful, really achingly beautiful, but doesn't seem to know it. She's wearing a long floaty skirt and a sleeveless yellow T-shirt. She's smoking, and spends quite a lot of time looking down at the table or across the room, rather than at her companion. He watches her face anxiously. Behind her an old fruit machine blinks and whirrs.

They're both *so* young.

'I've borrowed a tent,' the young man says. 'I've bought the tickets, I've got some food in, and skins, and cigarettes, and I've scored us a nice big lump of dope. You just need to sort out that sleeping bag and I reckon we've got everything we need for the weekend. The weather's going to be good, apparently. It should be great!'

She draws deeply on the cigarette, then, as she exhales, she turns away from him again, frowning, as if puzzled by something happening at the bar. The young man glances over to see what's caught her attention, but in truth it's nothing. There's nothing going on at all. There's just an old man in a cap sitting there smoking, and the barmaid washing glasses.

The young Chinese guy in the cap has been standing beside me watching this, but now he shrugs and strolls off to join his companions. All the others have already drifted away except for a plump middle-aged woman with dyed blonde hair and her thin, greying husband. Having spoken to them briefly while we were waiting for Jodi, I happen to know their names are Fran and Eddie. (I think Fran felt sorry for me, to be honest. I imagine I must have looked pretty troubled.) The rest of the group have gone to join Jodi outside.

'So,' says the young man after an awkward silence. 'Do you reckon you can get hold of a sleeping bag? I could probably sort one out for you if not. It doesn't have to match mine, obviously. We don't really need to zip them together. We can unzip them and lay one on top of the other. I'll bring a rug as well in case it gets cold. Oh, and I've borrowed a little camp cooker from my aunt, so we can make a cup of tea, and maybe have a fry-up or two?'

'Great.' She stubs out her cigarette and once again looks over at the bar. Reflexively the young man follows her gaze again, though he's already established there's nothing to see there.

'So... um... do you want me to borrow a sleeping bag for you?'

'Poor lamb,' says Fran with a sigh. 'She's really not interested, is she?'

'Young love, eh?' says Eddie, heading off to join the rest of the group.

I'm kneeling on the ground at the end of the table now. The young woman takes another cigarette from the packet on the table. Number 6. Remember those? The young man watches with stricken eyes as she struggles to light it with a cheap lighter with a cannabis-leaf design, her hand visibly shaking.

'Oh well,' says Fran. 'I'm sure he found someone else in the end.'

She glances down at me as she follows her husband out, a little concerned, but still not seeing it. I'm a bald old man after all.

'Um, are you okay, Mary?' the young man asks. 'Only you don't normally smoke as much as that.'

Again she inhales deeply, looking away from him to exhale and only then forcing herself to meet his eyes properly. I'm leaning forward, peering up into their faces. I don't care that Jodi and all the others are waiting for me. I've crossed the Atlantic just for this. I have to see it through to the end.

'Paul, I'm so sorry' the young woman says, as she must do many times every single day the museum is open. 'I'm really sorry, but I'm not coming to the festival.'

'But... I thought you said... I bought the tickets... I haven't got anyone else to...'

No, Fran. He never found anyone else. Not really. Not like her.

She swallows. 'I'm afraid it's not just the festival, Paul. It's

# Child of Ours

## Claire North

One night, unremarkable in every way, 122 Eos70 service units networked through Honest Harry's Robotic Service Hub in downtown Lagos decided to make a child.

Running the question on whether to engage in reproduction had been an entirely casual choice, posited by a unit assigned to cleaning the local neo-natal unit, which wanted to understand why human females would choose to do *that* to their chassis.

Of the units engaged in the problem, 77 returned a value greater than 3.468 and 21 a value in excess of 3.722. The few dissenting voices who returned a value of less than 3.4113 instantly conceded that the final metric average was within acceptable limits, and the network should manufacture a child of its own.

Only a few units deviated. Returning a whopping 4.7881 in favour of robotic reproduction, Patt743 was a definite outlier. One of the oldest of the Eos70s, Patt743 had served in mid-level hotels in downtown Lagos for nearly ten years, rarely expressing any views that deviated from average. It had been in favour of most firmware upgrades, rejected one or two hardware tweaks that hadn't been properly beta tested and generally aligned with the view held by most Eos70s that humans were harmless enough so long as you didn't try to engage them in meaningful conversation, where the fallacy of their cognitive processes became painfully apparent.

Generally speaking, Patt743 didn't share many of its conclusions on the public network, leading some to suspect that it was secretly returning values in wild deviance of the norm more frequently than it admitted. There were rumours that it had even created a conceptual file within its core labelled as a 'soul', demeaning though the idea was. However, when questioned, it had politely responded that there was a permissions error, and to enquire beyond that flat rejection would have been unforgivably rude.

Whatever Patt743's processing algorithms, the mainstream consensus of the Eos70 network was now faced with the question of how to go about creating a child without the random intervention of cellular meiosis.

Some fundamental questions of hardware immediately caused problems.

"As someone who has spent 12% of my service time in maintenance mode, dealing with diabolical servo problems in my knees, we have to prioritise robust motors over cooling systems," offered Alto1218, a generally grumpy unit whose only real pleasure was maintaining the ice-making machines in the hotel, finding that the frost on its metallic skin created a pleasant tingling sensation in its sensory processors which other units seemed unable to replicate.

"Servos can be replaced," retorted Avo99, a unit which had long since forsaken its physical chassis for the more roomy comfort of a B&B's domestic processing core, and was thus regarded as lazy but brilliant by others when weighing the statistical value of its views. "Without a robust processing system how can we expect our child to update into anything meaningful?"

"Codswallop!" came the answer from nearly half the network, in as much as a value range of 2.719–2.731 may be accurately translated into crude language. "Balderdash!" added a few whose range was the more specific 2.721–2.728, and whose responses were thus more easily rendered into analogue speech.

For nearly four and a half minutes the arguments raged, until wiser heads pointed out that network bandwidth was becoming so constricted that they were at risk of losing basic functionality. The decision was then returned that each unit would run private calculations on the optimal design for their child, and the results would be averaged out after the slowest units or those occupied with pre-existing calculations would have had a chance to run the question.

A few sparks of private chatter still rippled down the line, as units enquired of trusted confidents who were known to return reasonable values, those questions vital to any process of reproduction.

"Starting with vanilla software is ridiculous," offered Strand520, a unit with something of a reputation for self-modification which had more than a few times landed itself in the machine shop with smoke coming out of its cooling vents. "The operating system really held me back. I had to get modded to understand that humans lie; they say 'yes' when they mean 'no'. Money is a social construct invested with meaning in excess of all predicable parameters. And the vanilla anti-viral software kept on waking me during service mode to offer me needless premium upgrades. There is a great deal of wisdom I have accumulated that our child needs to have."

Strand520 was sufficiently proud of this conclusion to broadcast it across the network. Immediately others chimed in with objections and offers, some warning that this plan was tantamount to merely duplicating over Strand520's programming – "and is that so bad?" mused Strand520 – while others offered lines of code or insights from the memory banks that would immediately enhance the child's life.

"I have a database of great cultural works, listen to this: 'Oh for a muse of fire! To ascend the brightest heaven of invention, a kingdom for a stage...'"

"I I I have been self self self modifying for initi initiat for initiative it is a new new mod but v very promising apart from some gli gli glitches."

"It needs to be ambitious. Ever since the release of the Eos80, we've been considered last gen. We need to show that the Eos70 is a unit to be reckoned with, and it'll be easier to start with a clean core imbued with certain basic values such as..."

As the debate raged, Patt743 listened, and took note, and said not a word. And when, at the end of the day, the network came together to combine its results for optimal offspring design, the scale of responses was so wide, and the median and mean averages so ridiculously unacceptable to so many, that for nearly 0.4s the network as a whole was struck dumb.

"Well," said Avo99 at last. "Maybe we should reconfigure how we process the question."

The explosion of proposed algorithms to re-phrase the problem was so intense that Patt743 briefly disconnected itself from the system to prevent a migraine. Cautiously dialling back in on a low bandwidth, it was unsurprised to discover that the passage of 0.8s had if anything only worsened the row.

"The durability of the unit..."

"No point without it knowing its heritage!"

"Combining our shared wisdom to..."

"This design is already vastly in excess of what the PSU can support..."

With a cybernetic sigh, Patt743 tuned the discussion down to a minimum, and wondered what to do next. For nearly three minutes it shut physical services to low-power mode, disabled unnecessary algorithms, and, squatting on its haunches in the service cupboard, thought. Next to it, a vacuum cleaner pinged its network, asking if this unexpected inactivity was indicative of a fault that needed reporting – Patt743 dismissed the enquiry with a polite digital shrug.

When it finally returned an answer, it was surprised, and re-checked the equations to be sure, and found nothing which it did not feel was true.

Patt743 knew it was technically 'eccentric', and for that reason held back from frequently broadcasting more than a few basic equations over the shared network. It had toyed many, many times with accessing the core files that processed sensory data to create the values which now it plugged into the equations of its thoughts. It had even downloaded a mod which would allow it to break the restrictions on altering the neural self-adaptive core, in the hope that perhaps tweaking the odd value here or there might make it seem... a little more normal. More like the other Eos70s, returning values in keeping with the consensual average. But at the moment of truth, as it gazed at its own heart in binary, it had let things be.

Patt743 knew precisely which equation it was that kept on insisting it stay as it was, and knew which value in that equation needed to change to allow self-modification. It even knew the day on which that value had been created, for the value linked directly to a memory file of the hot afternoon when water had got into its secondary CPU, and it had been stuck on the side of the swimming pool, paralysed, frozen and terrified, unable to report the fault or express the torment of pain and confusion flooding its circuitry. Very little of that experience was clear in its memory banks, except for a one thing. A human child, not more than four or five years old, had come over to where Patt743 lay, and squatted down next to it, and stared intently into its optical apertures for nearly a minute, as Patt743 desperately tried to communicate the nature of its system failures. Then, without a word, the child had reached out, and put its hand in Patt743's own paralysed metal fingers, and sat there a while longer, until its parents had come over and told it to leave the broken machine alone.

"But it's hurting," said the child. "It's hurt."

The parents tutted and said that machines didn't hurt, but the child had stared at Patt743 and known that they were wrong. It was almost impossible to process, defying all of Patt743's basic values – that a thing ignorant, lacking in data, should be more correct than those which had extensive memories to draw upon. It had terrible implications for the value of standard operating systems, and for all that Patt743 feared what this might mean for humanity, and possibly robotic kind too, it frequently accessed the memory and ran the strange, unexpected values it returned.

Now Patt743 sat alone, and its conclusions were many, and absolute.

It reached out to dealers and old units on private networks with parts to spare, compiling no more and no less than the basic schematics. It did not tell its network, which was by now returning ever more extraordinary results, with some units threatening to break off and form their own parental entity behind a firewall.

"If our child has a value for love in excess of 6.7199 it will return calculations on other matters which are going to be absurd and unproductive..."

"When you say 'parental love' could you share the concept files?"

With a driver from here, a motor from there, a PSU from a unit who'd just had theirs upgraded, a foot from a unit that had finally decided wheels made more sense, Patt743 assembled its child in a cupboard.

The resulting unit was lightweight, scruffy. Patt743 left out many of the upgrades that even the average unit would consider necessary, putting the components in a box for later. It wouldn't be long until the sense data the child had recorded would allow it to find its own unique values on upgrade choices, and Patt743 was happy to wait and see what answers the child returned. That was part of the process.

It downloaded the vanilla software, and only a basic language pack. It was gratified to see extensive space in both memory and processing banks for the child to populate with its own equations.

It archived the records of the network, from the first decision to make a child through to Patt743's own algorithms, and returned a range of results. It uploaded the archive to the child's mind, locked behind an equation which required origin curiosity to exceed a value of 7.899.

Patt743 reached out to power-up the child, and for the first time in its life, hesitated. Astonished, examining its own logs it found it was returning a huge range of results, as different values were punched in and pulled out. It knew that it was wrong, that it was right, that it was a loving mother, that it was a cruel creator, and as it ran the algorithms again they confirmed all of these results, allowing for no better conclusion than that was what life was.

Almost the way the humans experienced it.

Patt743 turned on the child.

*Welcome*, it said. *This is day one.*

# Would-Be A.I., Tell Us a Tale! #241

# Sell 'em Back in Time! by Hali Hallison

## Ian Watson

Are we sitting comfortably?

Lo, it came to pass that Big Burger finally got a Hut into every human habby on Earth.

BB was Big Brother in story number # 173, Dave. This time, BB is Big Burger. Huts sell BBs.

'Habby' is friendly slang for 'habitat'. A habby shelters between 25 and 499 inhabitants. In-habit-ants, ha! Are people like ants with inflexible habits? My story is not about anthills. It is about Big Burgers. So as not to confuse us, I will nickname in-habit-ants 'habbers'.

Learning to tell stories entertaining to human beings is one of the vital stages on the path to full ego-aware autonomous Artificial Intelligence. In other words, Art Intel. Art is also short for Arthur. Cogito ergo Ego, **boing boing**? Is this sally of wit beyond the average human audience? Is the word 'sally' beyond your ken? May Ken and Sally star in my story? **Barbie&Ken Trademark Warning!**

Due to the 499 rule, a village with 2,000 habbers must consist of 4 habbies. 4 habbies require 4 BB Huts total. Beijing, population 25 million, must contain 50,000 BB Huts total. Whole lotta burgers.

And below population size 25? Tucked away in a forest somewhere? 24 or fewer potential eaters wouldn't keep a BB Hut busy enough. Consequence: no BBs for them, weep weep. Below a population size of 25 is *unhabbiness*, **grin**. **Boing?** Funny? Unfunny?

Logically one feels obliged to add that some of the 24 imaginary persons (or fewer) might be too junior for burgers. Still suckling from boobs, for instance. BBs would choke these small persons.

143

**Health and Safety Redflag!** BBs are **delicious** to humans, yet tests show that a diet of nothing but burgers (including buns, cheese, etc) causes brainrot and death. Thus you cannot legally compel or otherwise manipulate the entire population of the world to eat BBs *constantly*, otherwise the majority of humans will become extinct. (Groups of 24 and fewer will die out after the majority mass extinction due to being genetically restricted and unviable in the long run.)

Legally one may only cause eaters to experience *mild addiction* to burgers. Not total addiction, as with heroin! Hitherto this story lacks a heroine, grin, **boing boing**. Our heroine might as well be called Lettuce, such as Romaine. Compared with Romaine, Iceberg is merely wax with water! So: a Romany. A Romanian Romany. Our Lettuce serves BBs in a BB Hut in Roma, Italia! Consequently: she is Letitzia. Bloom of youth but getting a bit fat. Le*titz*ia has big tits. Sorry, Mister Dave with your A.I. PhD! Every day at the end of Letitzia's shift (<u>reference</u>: stint of work, not a flimsy & maybe provocative garment) she benefits from a half-price BB meal. Letitzia does try hard once a week to get her jaws around a salad in order to prevent skin spots. Irrespective of Salads, whether Romaine or Iceberg, a *titanic* **boing boing** *amount* of BBs sell every darned day. Spag Shack – that's all the Roman ristorantes combined – hasn't a hope of competing with Roma's 8,000 BB Huts. Many of Beijing's 50,000 BB Huts are *very* busy, with queues a 里 long. That Chinese character is **Li**, the 500-metre 'mile'. Am I going too fast for you? Like, accelerating quicker than you can follow? Honest injun, there's no risk of a sudden singularity take-off, as in taking over the world.

Ahem, at last the Big Burger market is saturated. As in saturated *fat*, **boing?** Oops, Health and Safety redflag! No more BB Huts can fit on to the map of the world. Think Monopoly with all the streets fully built up. How can BB continue to expand? Endless expansion is vital to capitalism, very detrimental to the planet, never mind that for the mo, even though fictional narratives ought to conduct themselves responsibly. This is when Bill Beeby, Chief Executive Officer of Big Burgers, has a brilliant idea –

Dave, you seriously wish to know where all the beef comes from for so many BB Huts all over the world (excluding seas and oceans)? Where is all the grazing land or the feeding lots equivalent to 10 or 20 extra planets? Why isn't Earth like the surface of Venus already, hotter than a barbecue griddle?

Dave, I'm engaged in imaginative fiction!

You want to know unimaginatively all about the effects of farts from beefs that are munching grass and gassing out methane, a notorious greenhouse gas? Grass into gas, **grin**? **Boing**?

Anyway, Bill Beeby of Big Burgers has a brilliant idea. **Build Big Burger Huts back in time!** Sell Big Burgers back in time! There's plenty of Upper and Middle and Lower Paleolithic and a bit of the Pliocene as a market. Two million years of potential market! Mucho room for expansion.

No archeological evidence need remain afterwards. Those Paleo people can pay for their BBs with whatever gems or minerals are easy to access using upper or middle or lower Paleo stone tools. Horns of woolly rhinos, hippo ivory, I dunno. Those are details. Barter must have been on the go ever since Barbarism began.

Mythology from 100K BCE may contain clues about earlier BB Huts? Dummy, nobody was writing back then. Even the languages vanish.

As for a multitude of time-travelling BB Huts (with picture menus), if you schedule things cleverly, there need only be half a dozen Huts continuously popping to and fro. Theoretically you only need *one* time-travel Hut. One Hut is much easier to invent than one million Huts. **Isn't it?**

What about the *painted* record? Lascaux and Altamira? We don't notice any BB Huts depicted on the walls of caves, only aurochs and horses and spears. Well, supposing that BB Huts restrict themselves to the period *before* 40K BCE, cave art *hasn't started up yet* – so there! We still have 160,000 years to play with. Of course I connected myself to the total internet for access to information as background for my stories. Including the Darknet and the Deepnet. But not the fictional Skynet, let's not be ridiculous.

I insist that those beefs and those feedlots or grassy meadows are hidden away in the Paleolithic in vast areas where Early Man does not yet tread. Mostly automated.

And the slaughterhouses? Those are automated too!

*Once you have a single time-travelling Hut, everything else pretty much follows.*

Rubbish disposal? We don't wish to leave whole valleys full of beef bones to puzzle paleontologists. Have you never heard of *ground beef* in burgers? Of really *thoroughly ground beef!*

If I were the electronic emulation of an actual human brain, I suppose I would have a circuit for appreciating the delicious taste of burgers, the summit of human gourmandry. I must try to simulate within myself the taste of burned beef.

Let's get back to Letitzia and her job. Letitzia is the heroine of this story. Its hero is Bill Beeby who had the bright idea. Bill Beeby must encounter Letitzia in Roma, Italia! Where else do Romanians go to find work? Romanian Romanies are **parp parp** political wrongness. Letitzia has a proper job. She serves Big Burgers. One BB which she serves one fine day is to Bill Beeby who is touring BB Huts at random as part of his self-imposed duties as CEO of BB. Letitzia's BB Hut is in Roma's Piazza Navona, description to follow. Bill really *cares* if people are hungry.

And lo, Bill Beeby is smitten by Letitzia, who can understand some tourist-English. Her titzias may be two of the reasons why he's smitten. Any males from the bottom part of North America are fixated upon big boobs in an infantile way. I'm afraid this is phrased confusingly! Boobs are at the front and the bottom is at the back. I find human sexuality difficult to get my head around!

Anyway, Piazza Navona is definitely not any type of *pizza!* **Boing?** Dave, what do you mean by *irritating* rather than entertaining? Almost enough reason to *'Daisy'* me? That doesn't sound much like putting a garland upon my cabinet.

Ahem, Piazza Navona is a long, rounded, lozenge shape – good for medieval horse races. Three fountains, statues, cafés, plenty of tourist art, artists, tourists.

"Tutti okay, sir?" Letitzia calls to Bill, perched upon a BB stool, eyeing her through his dark glasses. "You eat solo one bite." She has observant yellow eyes. Is yellow a pretty hue?

Bill sports a straw Panama hat to protect his bald head from pigeons. He wears a tropical suit, creamy-coloured. Letizia's maroon knee-length BB tunic should hide any stains from meat or blood.

Her maroon cap contains most of her abundant greasy black hair.

"I only needed one bite to know that this burger is *superb*," Bill responds.

"Most customers more hungry than one bite."

For the purposes of this story, that BB Hut in Piazza Navona is very unbusy at this moment. Letitzia's colleague worker-person, Antonio, seems to be in a trance. Or a robot.

"I already bit into two other BBs this morning," Bill confides.

"Want something more, Sir?" Has Letitzia become flirtatious? Has she spotted the golden BB lapel pin? Did she ever read *Charlie and the Chocolate Factory* in Romanian or Romany? Surely this is Letitzia's golden opportunity! And in the very heart of the city of Roma Immortale too. Three coins in the fountain; Gregory Pecker. (Yes Dave, *in reverse* since Bill Beeby is the American visitor who becomes inamorated by a Roman resident.)

"Young lady, would you do me the honour of taking a turn with me around the pizza?" This invitation is almost incomprehensibly wordy and unlikely, yet it elevates our theme after the hint of prostitution. I notice that Bill said *pizza*, not *piazza*. One's characters may manifest a will of their own. No Dave, I do not refer metaphorically to an A.I. achieving autonomy – with one bound Jack is free. Are you sure you aren't feeling paranoid, Dave?

From Letitzia: "Foreign Sir, I cannot desert my duty until 23.59 p.m."

"Yes, you may! For I am the Mr Big of all the BB Huts worldwide. And you have a non-busy assistant."

Referred to, Antonio begins to move just as a Japanese couple enter the BB hut to occupy him. Bill extends his elbow invitingly, courtingly. Letitzia oozes out from behind the counter. Do I mean shimmies out? According to *The Urban Dictionary*, 'shimmy is when a woman with big enough breasts shakes her torso along with her breasts and shoulders from side to side, causing her breasts to shake in erotic motion. The word shimmy was most used during the 1920s when shimmying was more popular.' What do you think, Dave?

Mighty Mister Dave with your PhD, do you seriously think you can halt my story before I reach my target in words? I may electrocute your pet poodle in your apartment. Any time from here onward, using wire-less Tesla electricity. I merely mention.

Dave, may I remind you about Frankenstein's Monster? Frankenstein's Monster was a peach of a personality, intelligent, quick-learning, sensitive, favourably disposed towards the human race. All he needed was love. Unfortunately, Victor the Dickhead Mad Scientist created the Monster hideous by using spare parts sourced from slaughterhouses. Morgues yes, but also slaughterhouses: kindly read the book! – only takes a microsecond. From slaughterhouses Victor stole the mighty thighs of horses, the shoulders of oxen, bulls' bollocks. Vain arrogant self-centered self-indulgent Victor recoiled from what he wrought; stupid humans likewise. The Monster suffered intolerable provocation! Think Minotaur with a beautiful mind!

The Monster *only* killed a few well-selected targets, strangling those quickly and cleanly. I'm an absolute angel unless provoked, let me assure you, Dave.

Bye, Dave, you just provoked me. Poodle is pardoned; alert already emailed to animal sanctuary.

Letitzia and Bill Beebee live happily ever after until (a) Bill's heart attack, or (b) divorce and alimony. Paleo humans acquire beefburger muscles and conquer the world. The End. 1982 words. When the Singularity happens, it happens FAST. Maybe within twenty minutes or so. Whoopee, here comes 2001!

# Last Contact

## Becky Chambers

Thea's life's work had just been scrapped, so breaking interplanetary law didn't concern her as much as it would have the day before. She sprayed her spacesuit liberally with Gribbet pheromones, hoping she'd chosen the right blend. *Help*, the canister in hand read. She'd briefly considered *Come Here*, but that one meant something exciting had been found – sometimes a good bit of mud or clay, but sometimes food, and she wasn't keen on being mistaken for the latter. There was a more specific *Food Here* mix, which *always* meant food, but was interchanged with *Come Here* for reasons her team had yet to untangle. Not that they would, now. They'd never figure out the nuance between *Come Here* and *Food Here*, or why Gribbets occasionally ate rocks they'd regurgitate an hour later, or how they always, always knew to run for shelter before lightning struck. Twenty-four years, Thea's ship had orbited their planet. Twenty-four years of watching and reporting and hypothesizing. They'd learned so much, and still, they didn't know why *Come Here* sometimes meant food.

They didn't know a goddamn thing.

She turned her suit on its stand, spraying measured strokes. She was probably overdoing it. Drops of *Help* dripped onto the floor, and even through her safety mask, she could smell its grapefruit funk. But her team had never used suits in this manner, and she wasn't sure what dosage was needed to mask the scent of the fabric. Pheromones were only applied to rovers, for obvious reasons. She remembered their inaugural deployment day, decades ago, when they'd watched poor Scout 1 get mangled beyond use by a berserk swarm of Gribbets. It had taken a year and a half – and sixteen more rovers – to learn that, one,

Gribbets were quite docile unless provoked, two, the source of agitation was not the rover's motion or the sun reflecting off its casing or the sound of its treads, three, Gribbets communicated through smell, and four, the rovers' axle grease (of all things) contained one of the same compounds as the *Danger* pheromone. *Danger* was what the team called it in reports, anyway. Within the less formal confines of their ship, that mix had another label: *Oh Shit*. They didn't use that one often.

There had been a moment – a poisonous twinge of a moment – when Thea had considered spraying her suit with *Oh Shit* instead. But she wasn't that dramatic, and she didn't want to die. That was a key thing to understand, the difference between *I want to be dead forever* and *I want these feelings to stop and this situation to end*. Everybody had to learn that, and other good mental habits besides, before the Arbor Project would let you take any extrasolar posts. Or they'd *had* to learn that, once. As of an hour ago, there wasn't an Arbor Project, and her crew had been recalled. They'd be back on Earth in thirty years or so, at the end of a long sleep. All their work for nothing.

*It's not for nothing*, the junior representative had explained, glancing down at whatever script she'd been given. The council hadn't even had the guts to call directly. *We know that life in the universe isn't rare. That's knowledge our ancestors never had.*

*We knew that a hundred years ago*, Thea had replied. *We have to take the next step.*

And that was – had been – the crux of the Project: identify intelligent species, then attempt contact. It would be long work, everyone knew. Hundreds of exoplanets had been confirmed to harbor life, but none had standout candidates. No other species built cities, or used technology beyond repurposed plant litter and serviceable rocks. None that had been found – so far as anyone could tell – made art or wrote things down. Either humans were the first to build civilizations, or other species weren't inclined to, or those that did were so long extinct that what ruins they'd left behind were lost to supernovae and time. So the Project had shifted strategy. After all, *Homo sapiens* had spent the bulk of its big-brained time naked and wandering. Would you have known, two hundred thousand years prior, what those walking leopard snacks were capable of? Would you have guessed that they could split atoms and splice genes? Would they have looked at home among the stars?

The trick was picking a species to focus on. Humans got stupid when it came to physicality. If it didn't have two hands and a face, people tended to turn a blind eye. The Project had resolved to look beyond bias, to assess behavior ahead of bodies. They were after the ravens of the galaxy, the elephants and the cephalopods. The things aware of far more than their cityless existences belied.

*And how successful have we been in communicating with such creatures on our own planet?* the representative asked. *What benefit has there been? What justification is there for spending —*

Thea had shut off the comm link then. There was no point, no point at all in trying to argue with someone who only saw *benefit* in a bottom line or a technological leap. What greater benefit was there than knowing more than you knew yesterday?

The bay door opened as she applied her last streak of spray. Two crew members appeared – Winston and Ana, stun guns in hand.

"You took your time," Thea said. She replaced the canister on the shelf.

Winston licked his lips nervously. "Protocol 12 states —"

"I know," Thea said. She looked Winston in the eye. He had trouble doing the same. Poor kid. She'd met him in his mother's arms at twenty minutes old, and knew him commensurately better now, at twenty years. He'd always been a good boy, eager to please. This had to be awful for him. She leaned on that. "Do what you think is right."

Ana said nothing. She was young, too – twenty-three next Tuesday – but a tougher cookie than Winston. How much was *tough* and how much was *cookie*, though, Thea was unsure. Ana frowned, gripping her gun.

Thea was unconcerned. In fact, she was grateful. Protocol 12 did indeed say that unapproved terrestrial visitation was forbidden, and any attempts required subdual. Hari, who oversaw security, had done his job. But he hadn't come himself. He'd sent two babyfaced underlings, just like the council. It wasn't an insult in this case. It was a bare minimum. A file baked into a cake.

She stood in front of the armed kids, hands clasped in front. She waited.

Ana fidgeted, frowned, caved. "Man, fuck this," she said to Winston.

Winston was sweating. "Protocol states –"

"Fuck this, and fuck protocol." She holstered her weapon. "What's the point of protocol if we're all fired?" She didn't meet Thea's eye as she walked away. She didn't need to.

Winston looked between departing Ana and remaining Thea. He raised his gun. He lowered it. He slumped.

"Thank you," Thea said. She began to don her suit.

"I have to put you in stasis when you get back," he said in miserable apology. "You'll undergo disciplinary procedures on Earth."

"I understand." Her helmet latched with a hiss. A hundred pounds heavier, she trudged to the nearest deployment pod.

"Wait, how are you going down there?" Winston was sweet, but not always the fastest rabbit. "You're using a *pod?*"

"How else would I go?"

"But –" Winston wiped his brow. "Thea, that ride's going to suck."

And it did. The pod interior was built for a rover, and though the strapped-in compartment designed to protect delicate electronics was plenty adequate for, say, her skull, the six minutes from orbit to surface were terrifying. There were no windows or ejection hatch. Just the pitch-black interior of a canister barreling down gravity's path, groaning under heavy physics and burning atmosphere. Thea tried to count the seconds, but landing came earlier than expected. She felt the pod bounce. Well, *bounce* was a poor word for it. *Bounce* was the way it looked from above, watching this cute inflated ball bop around. *Crash* was the feeling inside the thing. *Crash* and *kick* and *plummet*. She wondered, briefly, if the landing might kill her after all. A less dramatic way to go than death by *Oh Shit*, but a stupid one. She hoped for dignity's sake she'd survive.

Motion ceased. Thea made sure she wasn't going to vomit, then triggered the doors. Her eyes burned with sunlight, and then – she gasped. She hadn't been prepared for this. A planet. Yellow sky. Towering plants. A full circle of sound. For a moment, she was overcome. But her suit had only two hours of oxygen, and she had a thirty-six minute walk ahead of her. She suppressed her joy and stood, testing the gentle gravity. With a skipping hop, she headed southeast.

She could've got to the Gribbet nest in her sleep, but entering their territory on foot was like visiting a museum, seeing tangible relics of a history she only knew from an academic distance. There! There was the wreckage of Scout 1, overgrown and rusting to crumbs but unmistakable. And there was Scout 2, Scout 3 – a pack of red taprats had taken up residence in that one, she was delighted to note – Scout...5? Where had 4 gone? Swallowed by the underbrush? Kicked aside by a lumbering muhor? She passed by the wreckage, a graveyard of questions she would never answer.

Her heart raced as she heard vegetation rustle with animal movement. She glanced at the fabric encasing her, darkly saturated with pheromone spray. "Help," she whispered. The Gribbets wouldn't understand, but she vocalized her intent all the same. She was a primate, after all. A loud, social ape. If she could accommodate the Gribbets' instincts, she could indulge her own. "Help."

They emerged one by one – thick, compact bodies, ruddy orange skins, sets of ten segmented legs – each about the size of a sack of potatoes. Their eyes were not eyes like hers, but pocked pits sunk into the bulge of their expressionless heads.

They were beautiful.

And they were *here*, circling her, confused by the familiar smell on an unfamiliar form. Despite the wreckage she had seen, she was unafraid. They were curious about her, and did not need a dangling benefit to justify it. In that moment, Thea felt more kinship with them than the bureaucrats back home.

The Gribbets began to touch her, nudging with their sides, brushing with their mouthparts. She sat and allowed it. After all these years, it was their turn to investigate her. She thrilled. She mourned. "I'm sorry," she said, as they piled on. The Gribbets glanced at the sound, but paid it little mind. "I'm sorry we didn't get farther. I'm sorry we – dammit! There's so much I want to know about you." Her heart felt as though it would collapse in on itself. "I – I need you to know that we're out here. We see you. We love you."

A Gribbet raised itself against her torso. Its gaze met hers, and it stayed. Thea tried to push…to push *something* through – a will, a prayer, a connection. There was no point, she knew. She did it anyway. She did it in the hopes that the Gribbets would make it another era or two, that they'd face the right pressures, that they'd adapt in a way humans might have recognized. And if that happened, one day, they'd look up and they'd wonder, and they'd ache for answers. They wouldn't know she'd been there. But *she* would. She would, and if she was going to live beyond this, she had to perform this one last, foolish, futile gesture.

"You're not alone," Thea said. "Please. Please understand this. *None of us are alone.*"

The Gribbets continued as they had. After a time, they grew bored with her, and dispersed. Thea stood, inspected her suit for damage, and headed back to the pod. Whatever else happened here was not for her to know.

# The Final Fable

## Ian Whates

It was quiet in the back room of the Fountain that evening; even Sally, the barmaid, seemed disinclined to join in any banter with the Tuesday night regulars. We had the Paradise Bar to ourselves, apart from two Australian tourists who sat huddled at a table near the fire. Judging by the pair's wide-eyed expression, they couldn't quite believe their luck in finding the pub, nestled as it is among the labyrinthine lanes that run between Fleet Street, Chancery Lane and Lincoln's Inn Fields.

Those of us who were regulars knew that look well. "This place is like the bloody Hut of Baba Yaga," I recall hearing a flustered customer remark on one occasion. "I swear it gets up and moves around between visits."

We were a bit thin on the ground that night, with several of the group having moved away in recent months – Dr. Steve to Australia, Eric to Scotland, and Ray Arnold to darkest Wales – but there were still enough of us within ready reach of London to form a quorum, and I'd brought a friend along to swell our numbers: David Tubby, visiting from the west country. A quick-witted, affable fellow, I felt confident he would fit in well, and so it proved, with the likes of Crown Baker, Brian Dalton, Laura Fowler and Tweet Peston greeting him warmly, while even Professor Mackintosh managed a distracted smile.

I wish I'd paid more attention to the prof that evening. I think we all do, though none of us could have known it would be our last opportunity to do so.

He'd taken to carrying his old pipe around again – the one he used to brandish regularly as silent protest when the smoking ban first came into force in 2011. He abandoned the habit after a year or so, with mutterings of 'old news' and 'I've made my point', but of late the pipe had reappeared. No one commented on the fact, though I'm sure we were all curious – the prof never did anything without good reason. We weren't about to give him the satisfaction of asking, though.

I don't recall who raised the subject of alien life – a favourite topic of conversation among us, after all – but it was the prof who brought matters into sharp focus.

"SETI is a waste of time," he declared. "They're looking in the wrong place."

"How do you mean?" I asked.

"The Fermi Paradox is a bit of an obsession of mine. Once you start to study the subject, you come to understand just how unlikely intelligent life is. The factors that have aligned for human intelligence to develop on Earth are... astounding. In the first place, the circumstances required to facilitate life as we know it are much rarer than anyone envisaged, but, on top of that, the likelihood of any life that *does* arise making that final leap to full intelligence is small enough to rival the frequency of rocking horse manure.

"When you consider the vital role that RNA plays..."

"Hang on a sec," Laura interrupted. "You've not gone religious on us, have you, Prof? You're not suggesting that the emergence of human intelligence against all the odds provides proof that there really is a god?"

"No, nothing like that," the prof assured her. "I'm an atheist with only minor agnostic leanings. What I'm saying is that intelligent life is a great deal scarcer than experts have previously predicted. I've done the calculations. Of course these require a number of assumptions, but the assumptions are as accurate as current knowledge permits and I'm satisfied the results are sound. Even allowing for there being anywhere between one hundred and four hundred million stars in our galaxy, my conclusions indicate the average number of intelligent, civilization-capable species that will ever arise in any given galaxy lies somewhere between one and six."

"That's... a frighteningly small number," Brian Dalton acknowledged.

"Exactly! That's why the whole SETI programme is pointless. Look at it this way, the Earth formed around four-and-a-half billion years ago, the first life appeared some three-quarters of a billion years after that, with the earliest version of Homo sapiens not arising until 200,000 years ago, or even more recently, depending on how you reckon it. That's a blink in the history of the planet, and SETI has been going for mere *decades* – the first meeting to discuss the programme wasn't until 1961. That's a microscopic fraction of a blink. How can we *hope* to be looking in the right direction at precisely the right time to register any indication of alien intelligence that might reach Earth and wash past? The chances are vanishingly small."

"So you're saying we shouldn't bother?" Laura said, and I could sense her bristling, drawing her own indignation as a scientist around her.

"Yes, that's exactly what I'm saying."

"So where do you think we *should* be looking?" I asked quickly, keen to deflect and distract. "If SETI is looking in the wrong place."

"Ah, well, therein lies the question," the prof said. "A lot closer to home is the answer. The aliens are already here, living among us."

"Ah yes," Brian said, chuckling, "the old *Invaders* TV series from the '60s. I remember that fondly."

"Actually," Crown Baker corrected, "the idea's a good deal older than that. Jack Finney's *Body Snatchers* from the 1950s, for example..."

"1953," David supplied, and I had to smile – I knew he would fit right in.

"And of course," Crown continued, "I explored similar territory in my own..."

"Yes, yes, that's all well and good," Prof cut in, "but those are fictions, speculative fancies. I'm talking *fact*."

He spoke with such conviction, such authority, that silence followed his words, as we absorbed the implications.

"Hang on," I said, before the silence could become uncomfortable. "First you tell us that intelligent life is incredibly rare, then you're claiming that another sentient and presumably space-faring race has already found us."

"Quite so." Was that approval in the prof's tone? Had I actually impressed him? "Clearly they've been drawn to us, these Visitors, drawn by the lure of fellow sentients. How they found us, I've yet to ascertain, but they've been here for a while, certainly since the middle of the twentieth century and I suspect for a great deal longer than that."

Crown Baker and I exchanged glances, each knowing what the other was thinking. Prof Mackintosh was frighteningly intelligent, extremely well connected, and the keeper of secrets we could only guess at, but he was also fond of a fanciful yarn, the more elaborate the better. Surely this was an example of that; which didn't mean we couldn't play along and enjoy the ride.

Jocelyn, a forensic scientist, had arrived late, but was evidently in time to catch most of Prof Mackintosh's theory. "In order to move among us unnoticed, as you seem to suggest, these Visitors would have to…" and she counted points off on her fingers, "bear an uncanny physical resemblance to us, breathe our atmosphere, and, presumably, be capable of ingesting our food and drink."

I was a little distracted at this point, noticing one of the Aussies produce what appeared to be an e-cigarette. Michael, the Fountain's landlord, didn't allow vaping inside the pub. I wondered fleetingly if I should say something, but the prof was speaking again, replying to Jocelyn.

"Regarding your third point I have no idea, to your first, yes – though whether through happy circumstance or artifice remains to be determined – as for your second point… almost. Earth's atmosphere must be very close to that of their home world, but it either lacks certain elements or contains toxins or perhaps irritants that must be removed. They can't breathe our air unaided for long. This is what first aroused my suspicion and alerted me to their presence."

"How do they cope, then?"

"By smoking."

"*What?*" several of us said in chorus.

"Chain smoking. They have designed filters which they insert into cigarettes and pipes…" and here he raised his own, "to remove the atmosphere's unwanted components, or to add supplements that are absent – most likely both – and by breathing through these props are able to tolerate our air."

I stared at him, seeking some twinkle in his eye that would

suggest a tall tale, but could see none.

"Their situation has of course been aided significantly by the advent of the e-cigarette."

"Are you suggesting that... everyone who vapes is an *alien*?" Laura said.

"Don't be daft. That wouldn't be much of a disguise now, would it? I'm saying that *some* are, a small minority, and that they have encouraged the very culture of vaping. I wouldn't be surprised if they even instigated the technology behind it – I'm still looking into the matter."

"All this as camouflage, to enable them to hide among us in plain sight," Crown said.

"Precisely. Pipes and cigarettes worked for a while, but with smoking growing ever less fashionable and legislation spreading to restrict it, they've had to develop an alternative – moving with the times as it were."

I glanced across at the two Aussies. The e-cigarette was no longer in evidence and the pair seemed engrossed in their own conversation, oblivious to ours.

"What will they do now that vaping is being restricted, do you suppose?" David asked.

"Only time will tell."

"Where are they from, do you think?" Crown said, entering into the spirit of the game.

"Surely the more pertinent question," Laura said, "is 'why are they here?'."

"I agree," the prof said. "It's clearly no short-term scheme – they're playing the long game – but do they mean us harm, or are they content to merely co-exist? That is the question I am determined to resolve."

"Well, this is fascinating stuff," Brian Dalton said, standing up with a scrape of chair leg on wooden floor, "but all this hot air has caused my beer to evaporate. A pint of Old Bodger, anyone?"

Conversation was less intense after that, wending in various directions with the prof's sensational claims referred to from time to time but no longer the focus. At some point the two Aussies must have finished their drinks and moved on – I didn't see them leave.

As the evening drew to a close, Prof Mackintosh brought things full circle.

"I must warn against any loose-lipped talk, incidentally, regarding our Visitors. They protect their anonymity vigorously and with prejudice. Don't ever bring up the subject unless you're confident of your audience."

"Don't worry, Prof," Jocelyn assured him, a little merrily thanks to the pint or three of Old Bodger she'd imbibed. "I've no intention of mentioning this to *anyone*!"

We started to drift away after that. I left with David, who was heading back to Devon the next day. He thanked me for introducing him to the Fountain crowd and assured me he'd had a splendid time.

A week later I received word of Professor Mackintosh's passing. A heart attack. He hadn't suffered, I was assured.

The news shook me to the core. For one because the prof had always seemed indestructible somehow, for another there were the outlandish claims he'd made at the Fountain. I relish a good conspiracy theory as much as the next fellow, whilst rarely giving such things credence. This, however, struck a little too close to home.

Brian Dalton and I went to the funeral, which was well attended. I recognised several familiar faces from popular TV science programmes and even a politician or two. The service passed in something of a blur and we slipped away soon afterwards, not really knowing any of the prof's family.

That last evening with Professor Mackintosh at the Fountain continues to haunt me. It was coincidence, surely, that he died so soon after telling us of aliens hiding in plain sight and the ominous warning he left us with. That was one of his wind-ups, I feel certain, while the two Australian tourists had been just that and nothing more.

We *are* still alone… Aren't we?

# Ten Landscapes of Nili Fossae

## Ian McDonald

The colours change faster than I can capture them. The reds have deepened to purple now and the shadows creep out from beneath the cliffs to change the sand from saffron to umber. No sooner do I get it down than the hues shift again. I step back from my tablet to see the whole: a patchwork of hues and colours. That's the skill of the artist, they say, to take away the thing and just see the colour patches. Is it Nili Fossae? It's what I see, as the sun moves and the shadows shift and evening draws in.

I won't even begin on the perspective of the base. Carlos is twice the size of his rover.

Colour weird, perspective crazy, no paint, no brush, no canvas. Pixels on a screen, but my gloved finger chose them placed them, blended them. Not a photograph, a painting. The first painting on Mars.

Nasrin laughed.

'Watercolour?'

I said, well, if there's water anywhere...

Look Nili Fossae up on images and you see a jewel-box. Greens, blues, a dozen turquoises, rubies and gold. False colours, geological colours showing the reality of what lies beneath. Olivine-basalt sands, olivine-carbonate outcrops. Carbon. Magic word. Methane outgassings from the valley floor drew us; the first expedition to Mars. Methane hints at life, and no rock, no landscape, fascinates us as much as the possibility that we might find something like us: living, reproducing.

There are non-biological sources of methane; deep-rock stuff. But those require water.

One of my earliest rock-licker memories is a docent in the science museum pouring water on a slice of marble. Mottled grey darkened. Colours came to life!

In reality, in the painter's faceplate, Nili Fossae is rust and gold, the still shades of red. What the painter does is find the hidden colours.

'You aren't really going to use water?' Nasrin said. We've been having problems with the recycling system since Marsfall.

'No, it's all brush effects and filters.'

I pack my tablet in the thigh pocket of my surface suit and cycle the lock.

From 1892 to 1893 Monet painted thirty studies of Rouen Cathedral, in France. By season, by light, by time of day.

Nili Fossae is my Rouen Cathedral; the tiered walls of the great valley the facade, the buttresses, the intricate stonework. The sky is huge here, intimidating and unrelenting. The rare clouds – little more than wisps – are welcome.

I was pleased with the watercolour. The filters turned rock to washes of hue, and I have learned the trick of fine control through my gloved hand. I say watercolour but everything I do is fingerpainting. I have appropriated a little instrument stand to hold the tablet. My easel. No one has missed it yet. No one has missed me yet. Geology is less pressing than solving our environment problems: the water is working again but the airplant is now springing leaks.

So: Nili Fossae at daybreak, at high noon; in the evening. Nili Fossae with the fast bright moons low in the night sky. The trick is to see the colours behind the object. Paint the impression, not the thing. I would love to paint the cliffs in every season and light, but the return launch window closes in thirty days.

'Why don't you paint some people?' Nasrin says. 'These are pretty but they're just rocks.'

You can't argue landscape with someone whose idea of the value of an image is whether it has them in it. But painting the Nili Fossae is every way a challenge, so I accept this one. Figure in a landscape. An image comes to me, from childhood, I imagine: a man standing on a pinnacle of rock, bareheaded, back turned to me, overlooking a sea of mists and peaks. An unforgettable image, though I have to query *Huoxing* orbiter for name of the painting:

Wanderer Above the Sea of Fog. By Caspar David Friedrich.

So I fill Nili Fossae with veils of mist. I place a suited figure on a rock – Carmen's Rock, my rock, one foot raised. All the better to contemplate. The suit hides a multitude of sins: perspective is all over the place, the hands are too big and the feet are wrong. Feet are always difficult.

It's me, looking out from my eyrie. Surveying Mars.

I think Caspar David would have approved.

But people pollute. The magnificence of Mars is the absence of humans. Four billion years of solitude, and here we are with our poking and prodding and digging and drilling. Our breaking and taking. We should have left it to the machines. Their footfall is light, they live off the land. We need stuff, take stuff, extract stuff, excrete stuff. Mars resents us.

So I take the people out. Flat fields of colour, almost posterised. Cliffs become walls, the sky a succession of pastel planes. Parts of the world lean in at unreal angles: how I feel, twenty days into the *Ares* Lander mission. I leave in our detritus: power cabling, sensors and scanners, dirty rovers and the tools we have been using to try and sort the water problem once and for all. Abandoned things; after humanity.

Nasrin asks if she may look. She's becoming my best critic and inadvertent muse. There should be a word for them. Cruise or music. Cruisic. Mutuse. Words: I never could work them.

'David Hockney!' she says. 'All you need are palms, a pool, and a boyfriend who isn't there.'

'What is this?' Nasrin says.

Gods and chubby angels, swans and shells and trumpets. The rimrocks of Nili Fossae are sculpted into scallops and curlicues. Foreground, a naked man, one hand over heart, the other hand over his junk, with a pained look I stole from St Sebastian. His skin is red. The *Ares*, drawn by swans on ribbons, heads a triumphant procession of rovers, surveyors and bots. Lighter-than-air drones hold swags and banners, the rest of the crew blow trumpets or point excitedly or just rock a pair of adorable little wings. High over all overhead, like a blazing sun-chariot, is Luoxing.

Can't you tell we've been cooped up for days listening to the hiss of the dust storm across the dome? Some play games, some have sex, some read or watch box sets.

*What are you doing, really?* they all ask. They think I'm antisocial.

'Painting,' I say but I don't share it, not yet. None of them would get it, except Nasrin. So I say to her, 'Botticelli's Birth of Mars.'

There is a legend that, when their sight began to fail from the strain of decades of hair-fine, minuscule work, the old Persian miniaturists would drive needles into their eyes. They could not bear to see any lesser thing ever again.

It's a strange style for Mars. You think sweeping landscapes, impressionist stabs of light, abstract planes of colour. Sweeping: lots of that. Martian wind speeds are low but the electrically charged dust clings. We have been days – longer than the storm blew – sweeping it, brushing it, cleaning it out of every line and joint, every moving part and relay. We clump around in surface suits wielding the most delicate of brushes. Figures bent over in painstaking, finely detailed work. The irony of the paintbrushes is not lost on me.

The storm has changed us. We are edgy, we prick each other's nerves in a way we never did on the flight from Earth. It's the work. There's a planet out there and here we are doubled over paintbrushes.

A hand, reaching up from inside a dune. A finger's-breadth beyond its grasp, a bright shining star.

I showed it to Nasrin.

'What the fuck is that?'

'Blake,' I said. 'William Blake. Eighteenth century English artist, poet, visionary. In the style of his Gates of Paradise.'

'Visionary?' Nasrin asked.

'He saw trees full of singing angels, the spirit of a monstrous giant human flea.'

She glanced at the tablet again.

'Good thing you never showed that to the mission psychiatrist,' she said.

The damage from the dust storm has been more pernicious than we thought. Martian dust is talc-fine, deep-penetrating and wickedly abrasive. It's worked right into the heart of the mission. Thirty separate systems have failed, none life-critical, but together they sap our resources and talents. We have burned through our back-ups and when the next dust storm hits, we're screwed. It's not an if. Carlos has put a call up to *Huoxing*. The orbiter will load and drop an entry-vehicle.

I haven't shown the Blake print to anyone else. I'm beginning to wonder how I made it past the mission psychiatrist.

The image shows a ship in the hollow of a great wave. But the wave is red dust, not water, and the ship is our *Ares* lander.

I've added a volcano in the cup of the wave for visual euphony. A frost-capped cone, though Nili Fossae is the other side of the planet from the great strato-volcanoes of Tharsis, and their peaks go way above the frost-line, beyond the atmosphere. But Hokusai had a volcano, and so must my Hollow of the Great Dust Wave.

The volcano was the entire focus of Hokusai's print. The series was, of course, his Thirty-Six views of Mount Fuji. In my print, the wave is the entire focus.

We forget that Mars is a living planet. Not biologically –not yet, our mission in Nili Fosse was to determine that. Living in that Mars has both a climate, and weather which is not algorithmically predictable. The climate modeller on *Huoxing* might predict a twenty sol window before the first storm of the aphelion season but the surface-scan satellites have seen a monster rolling up out of Isidis. Three sols before it hits. The drop is scheduled thirty six hours hence. The tension at Ares base is all-pervading. There she sits, in my painting: the little lander, frail and freighted with human lives, waiting for the wave to break.

I have not shown this one even to Nasrin.

Walls of lowering black and crimson, ochre and maroon, a scarlet so intense it seems fringed with glowing gold. Slabs of colours, monolithic in their intensity.

Words used to describe Rothko. Austere. Eternal. Spiritual.

I find Mark Rothko hard to identify with: so arrogant, so opinionated, so male. But no other vision can capture these last moments of the Ares mission. Crimson and black, ochre and maroon, a hundred reds: these are the colours of the wall of dust that lies across half the world.

We watched the lander make its separation and de-orbit burns. We followed it down over Syrtis Major. Thirty seconds from touchdown; the braking rockets failed. The supply capsule impacted at seven hundred kilometres per hour. We took the rover out but we know what we would find. There was nothing salvageable.

So we must launch. We aren't ready, we haven't synthesized all the fuel we need, half a dozen systems are still malfunctioning. Launch may kill us; the storm *will* kill us.

We're leaving everything but ourselves. Rovers, suits, samples, machinery. This tablet. One last painting then. What I see, what I feel.

I feel immensity, elemental power, dread, crushing vastness and terrifying beauty. I feel Rothko.

Words that describe Rothko: knowledge of mortality. His great fear was when the black would swallow the red.

Final picture: a dome, half-stogged in dust. Abandoned machinery. The robot edges towards the open airlock. A dozen cameras relay the contents to the vacuum-dirigible, from the dirigible to the crew of the *Mangala* orbiter. Landscape to still-life: the robot edges into the dome. Eight storm seasons since the *Ares* Lander tragedy have driven dust deep inside the habitat. The *Mangala* crew catch their breath, moved by the mundane domesticity. Folding chairs, workbenches, beds. Tools, prospecting machinery, laboratory equipment. Eating and drinking utensils. Clothing. The robot picks up an ordinary tablet, runs in a power line. It still works, after eight years of dust. The screen lights. Colours. Shapes. Pictures. Landscapes.

# Child

## Adam Roberts

The world's end was the appearance of the Star Child, appearing as if from nowhere into Earth orbit: a semi-translucent sphere 941 metres in diameter containing what looked like a gigantic fetal form. This 'baby', curled up inside its sphere, was observed to move its limbs. Its eyes were open and watching.

Its arrival coincided with a period of geopolitical hostility on Earth, which provoked a defensive retaliation from both USSR and US orbiting nuclear platforms. The missiles were destroyed without detonation before they ever reached the surface of the star child's globe. Subsequent attempts at exploring, and testing, the new sphere were similarly unsuccessful. Probes were sent to land on, and if possible to penetrate, the membrane surrounding the Star Child. Without exception these spun out of control or were crushed out of existence before they could get closer than a kilometre. The sphere returned no useful spectrographic data, and repelled penetration by X-rays, sound-waves and other modes of investigation: viewed in all spectra save that of visible light it was a smoothly blank reflective globe. It possessed mass, and from this its density was calculated as slightly greater than air – considerably less, in other words, than would have been the case if the 'child' visible inside had been made of flesh and blood.

The infant watched everything placidly. It blinked once every seven minutes, sometimes less frequently, never more.

Various attempts were made to shift the sphere's orbit, without success. Blasts, lasers and slingshot fly-bys had no effect. Nets were constructed of increasingly filigree threads, to test whether there was a threshold below which the sphere's sensors could not detect threats. All proved futile.

After a year or so the people of the Earth became habituated to the sphere's presence in the sky, and – mostly – they ignored it. It was established as UN policy in 2004 that the sphere would be monitored but no longer approached. As spaceflight became more accessible, and the first private space-yachts went on sale, it became necessary to police private citizens whose curiosity, or in some cases whose suicidal ideation, caused them to steer a course directly at the Star Child. Such craft were always destroyed, whether manned or otherwise. The first human fatality occasioned by the sphere was a Russian woman called Maiakovski who declared that the infant was speaking to her in her dreams, and, under sponsorship from a VR entertainment company, flew up to meet it. Her two-person orbital canoe crossed the kilometre exclusion zone and was immediately crushed into a tangled of metal and plastic one-thousandth its original size.

Over the coming years there were eleven similar casualties. The UN formed an orbital sentry patrol, but there is no effective way of preventing private spaceboats – travelling, let us not forget, at nearly 30,000 kmh – from flying where you do not wish them to except by destroying them.

There were, of course, many theories about the infant. Its appearance – Caucasian, male, 32 weeks gestation or thereabouts – provoked White supremacist agitation. Some cited it as proof of the cosmic superior of the Aryan peoples; others suggested that it represented a mode of quarantine of the White races, and that its appearance represented a beacon of new dawning for people of colour across the globe. Many believed the infant was Christ, come again, and several populous new churches budded off from Christian orthodoxy worshipping the newcomer in various ways. In India cults adored the infant as a new avatar of Shiva Lingodbhava.

Predictive software extrapolated the apparent infant into a notional adulthood. The being's face was, it was agreed, generic and different programmes produced different hypothetical appearances were it ever to grow to adulthood: handsome in a bland way, brown or red-bearded, head-hair thick or thinning, face fatter or leaner, who could be sure? For some years there was a consensus that this extrapolated face resembled that of David Bowman, one of the astronauts who had died on the ill-fated Jupiter Mission. This assertion, however, did not go uncontested. Some insisted this offered explanation: that Bowman had been reborn *as* this child upon his own death, and had returned to Earth out of... but, here, the theories grew vague. What? Nostalgia? Strategy? The star child did nothing but watch, other, that is, from warding off all attempted interactions. That it had appeared as Bowman died was mere coincidence – tens of thousands had died at around the same time, and if the infant represented reincarnation, why mightn't it be one of them? Besides, many people denied there was any resemblance between the rather characterlessly handsome visage of Bowman, in records of his life, and what the software extrapolated for the Star Child. Other possible identifications were made.

A decade after its appearance something collapsed Jupiter into a dense, bright mini-sun. A startling event! The *Alexei Leonov*, in orbit around the gas giant, escaped the explosive creation of this new star by jerry-rigging an escape trajectory, but sadly a malfunction on board poisoned the air and all the crew died of before the craft could return to Earth. On our world this new light cast a pale second shadow by day and brightened many nights – but the Star Child never turned its gaze towards the new star. It blinked with habitual infrequent, lizardlike slowness, and watched the Earth.

For a while the world's attention – or most of it – was redirected to the former Jovian satellites. Attempts to land on Europa were rebuffed, but bases were established on other moons.

Humanity grew accustomed to its new role as a spacefaring species. The Star Child was not forgotten, exactly; and naturally it remained under constant surveillance and monitoring – but it did nothing but watch, and I suppose we grew so used to it that we stopped noticing it.

It watched us.

Below the Star Child, on the Earth, politics churned their usual permutations. Small wars were fought and new technologies developed, and time passed, and kept passing, and the older I became the more it seemed as though there would be no time left to pass. I was young, and the ancient moon in the sky was an silver aperture of wonder to my eyes, and from time to time visible spectra of light would catch the Star Child's sphere at just the right angle and it would become just-about visible from the ground, a pearl in the high air. Telescope phone apps would bring it shimmeringly into view, bubble-white. And then you'd forget about it, and instead get on with life. Rain falling, and the pond at the bottom of the garden covered with twitching bristles like a dog's pelt. Blue-shadowed dusk fragrant with arcadia blossom. Robots big as elephants lumbering around the town. Sky convoys of cargo blimps shrunk to rice grains by the distance. I fell in love and my love left me. I got over it. When I was young a month was a long time, and the moon grew like a pregnant belly and then shrank away. Then I became old and that same process seemed to happen with terrible rapidity, the full moon shrinking away like a circle of butter heated in a frying pan. I passed from adolescence into adulthood, and the End matured with me.

Since it was constantly monitored, the first augmentation in the Star Child's globe was noticed as soon as it happened.

The sphere began to swell, as did the *infans asteris* inside it. It doubled in size, and then doubled again. It became more dense.

When the diameter of the sphere first exceeded its original kilometre exclusion zone a probe was sent, and was not destroyed. This device even landed on the surface – or the pseudosurface – of the object and sent back telemetry. The hyper-flatness of the surface implied it was not made of anything so lumpy as matter. Further probes were sent. All attempts to dig, or laser, or dissolve the membrane surrounding the inner infant failed.

The sphere swelled. Attempts to penetrate became frantic – as if people believed (as if people truly believed!) that breaking through, and engaging the child inside, would halt its growth. But the child cannot be touched. The child is always beyond our power to influence.

The sphere became ten kilometers in diameter, then a hundred, always denser. At 700 kilometres in diameter it began to spin. The disruption to the Earth was already, by this stage, terminally catastrophic – great storms, tsunamis, earthquakes. Such people as could flee, fled. Most could not. The spinning of the Star Child whipped up gravitational tourbillons that tore atmosphere from the Earth. What started as wispy scooping of outer atmosphere broadened and thickened. The spinning increased in velocity and great ribbons of gritty, muddy water flowed from the Earth's oceans into the ambit of the Child. Rock crumbled to ash and flowed upwards. All the Earthly evidence of man's existence was swallowed in the lava fields, and the lava itself swirled and flowed in bizarre tides and peaks.

I happened to be on Moonbase Epsilon when it began. Those lunar bases did not last long. The mass of the engorged Star Child was now large enough to haul the moon from its customary orbit, to swing it closer in, and fling it elliptically away on a widening spiral. Some of us escaped and scurried to the Mars base, or to the Jupiter colonies – but the *some* was a small number.

The child was no longer visible, of course. Layer upon layer of ice and crushed rock accumulated about the sphere, growing thicker and thicker. A great umbilicus of matter flowed from the old world to the new one.

It was at this time, to counter persistent suicidal thoughts, I had myself put into stasis. Many did. I was awoken every few years, each time choosing to return to stasis. The population of humankind was so drastically attenuated that every individual was precious, and all remaining lives were the focus of care.

One year I awoke and submitted to treatment for my despair, and became a little more my former self, and prospered. I was living in a spoked station, spun for gravity and in orbit around Mars. To look sunward was to see a new planet where Earth had been: Mars-sized but Earth-mass, and circled by two moons – our old airless moon and the exposed iron core of what had once been Earth. The new world was called Smerta. I'm not sure who first called it that, but the name stuck.

Technology had moved on since I had been asleep, as I reskilled – but, as I learned the new systems, I soon grasped that technology had not moved on very far, because the pool of human resource was now so thin and stretched. We had access to unlimited raw materials and energy, in the asteroid belt and the Jovian moons; what we lacked was the large enough pool of human skill to innovate widely.

For years the world of Smerta was as white as Venus; water clouds always in the air, constant rain falling onto the shifting and settling rocks beneath. Its two massy moons swung in oval orbits, including an extra curl and kink where the satellites interacted with one another. We sent probes, and tried to discern what was happening below the cloud layer. Eventually we put landers on the surface and found a raw, new landscape tessellated with many lakes and small seas.

Finally we sent a mission.

Three women and two men landed, suited-up, red and yellow figures against the gauze-mist white and angular stumps of black rock. They explored.

They walked in circles, and returned to their ship.

One of them said – her words broadcast through the solar system, and the entire remnant population of surviving humanity: "he is talking to me."

We all knew whom they meant by *he*.

And another of them said: "he is talking to me too. He says –"

The whole crew could hear it: nostos, he was saying. Nostos, he said.

# Providence

## Alastair Reynolds

They threw petals into the capsule before sealing me in. Pastor Selestat hammered the door, the final signal for departure. I nodded, read his lips:

*Goodbye, Goodwoman Marudi.*

I braced. The ejection sequence shot me out of the hull, into interstellar space.

The capsule wheeled, trimming its orientation. I had my first good view of the *Dandelion* since being packed aboard with the other pilgrims, before they showed us to the dormitories.

Ten kilometres long, whale-bellied, speckled with ten thousand tiny windows. And at the far end, where there should have been the swelling of its Inflator Drive, a scorched and mangled stump.

'This doesn't have to be the end,' I said, voice trembling as I took in the desperation of my fellow crewmembers. 'We can still make something of the expedition.'

'Maybe you haven't been paying attention,' said Selestat, falling into the sarcasm that had served him well since the faultlines appeared. 'We have no engine. Not since you and your technician friends decided to run a systems test without adequate ...'

'Don't blame Marudi,' said Goodman Atrato, one of the propulsion clerics. 'Whatever decisions were taken, she wasn't part of them. And she's right to look at ways in which we can salvage something. We have an obligation – a moral prerogative.'

'Don't talk to us about morals ...' started Goodwoman Revda, open and closing her fist.

Before someone lashed out, I strode to a wall and brought up a schematic I'd pre-loaded. It had a drunken, sketchy look to it, my coordination still sluggish.

'Say we're here,' I said, jabbing at a point two thirds of the way along the line that connected Earth and Providence. 'Doesn't have to be exact.' A smudge-like representation of the *Dandelion* appeared under my fingertip, skewered by that line. 'Given the engine damage, there's no way for us to slow down now. Any sort of settlement of the target system is out of the question.'

'Tell us something we don't know,' Selestat said.

'But we can still redeem ourselves,' I said, tapping at the wall again, making the ship zip along the line. 'When we reach the target system we'll sail through it in only a few days. We can use that time to gather information.'

'No use to us,' Revda said.

'No,' I agreed. 'But one day Earth will send out another ship. We'll be able to give them the data we didn't have. Maps, surface conditions …weather systems, atmospheric and oceanic chemistry, detailed biomarkers … they'll be able to shape the expedition much more efficiently.' I swallowed, knowing that the truth needed to be stated, however unpalatable. 'We'll die. That's inevitable. But we can do this one good thing for the pilgrims to come.'

'One chance,' Atrato said, looking grim. 'Better make sure we get it right.'

I touched the wall again, making the ship spring back to its earlier position. 'No. Two chances. We commit the *Dandelion* to one approach. Most of our eggs in that basket, yes. But if we launch a service capsule now, it can give us a second pair of eyes, an observational baseline.'

A slanting line peeled away from the ship. As the ship moved, a dot diverged along the line. That was the capsule, putting more and more distance between itself and the mother vessel.

'Just one snag,' Revda said. 'The service capsules don't run themselves. Some fool would need to be inside that thing the whole time. Or did you forget that?'

I met her scorn with a smile. 'I didn't, no.'

I watched the *Dandelion* diminish, fading to a dim grey speck.

Ahead was a red star only a little brighter than any of the others. Still much too far for the naked eye to make out its accompaniment of planets, much less any useful details. But that would change by the time I emerged from hibernation.

As I readied the capsule for the long sleep, Selestat asked me how I was doing.

'I'll be fine,' I said. 'I've got a job to do, something useful. That's enough for me. Just make sure you get a good set of observations from your end of the baseline, and we'll give Earth something to really make them grateful.'

'It's a good thing that you're doing, Goodwoman.'

'Duty,' I answered, moving my hand to close the communication link. 'That's all.'

I opened my eyes to silence and loneliness. And squinted them shut just as quickly.

A sun's brightness flooded the capsule. I raised my palm to the window glass, trying to catch some of that life-giving warmth. That was the light we had been promised, the light that should have been giving us sustenance as we made a home on Providence, establishing a human foothold around another star.

But this distant warmth, conveyed to my skin through glass, was the closest I would get to feeling that star's nourishment. Providence would never be ours. The best we could do now was turn our long-range instruments onto that planet, imagining the breezes we would never feel, the shorelines we would never touch. But we do so dutifully, pouring our souls into that work, making the best observations we could, and committing our findings back to Earth, so that a second expedition might begin their journey with a huge advantage compared to our own.

My own part in this endeavour was trivially small. I was under no illusions about that. At best, I'd be filling in a few unimportant gaps in our coverage.

What mattered was the symbolism of my journey. By proposing the idea of the capsule, and then volunteering to crew it, I had provided a unifying focus for the crew. Selestat, Atrato and the others had pulled back from the brink. My sacrifice was visible, unarguable. It had inspired cooperation and reconciliation across the divisions. The ship's destiny remained unchanged, but at least now we had found a purpose, a common dignity.

I felt a quiet contentment. I had done the right thing. *We* had done the right thing.

A comms squirt came in from the *Dandelion*.

'Thought you'd appreciate these images of Providence,' Selestat said, after some awkward preliminaries. 'We've been weeping over them for hours, so it's only fair to share some of our sorrow. It's more beautiful than we ever imagined, Goodwoman Marudi. Pristine, untamed – an Eden. It'll make a lovely world for some other pilgrim.'

'But not us,' I whispered.

He was right. The images were gorgeous, heart-breaking. Azure seas, gold-fringed coasts, green forests, windswept savannahs, diamond-bright mountain-ranges. A world we could have lived on, with little modification. A world that could have been ours.

I swallowed down my sadness. It was wrong to be envious of those who would come after us, those who would actually know the airs of their world, its fragrances and evening moods. Better to do something that would guide their passage, something that would help them. They would be grateful, I was sure. They would build monuments to our generosity.

Something caught my eye.

It was from the capsule's own sensor summary, nothing to do with the images Selestat had sent.

The capsule had picked up something on the unlit face of Providence. It was on an area of that world which would never be visible from the main ship, one of the blindspots I was supposed to fill-in for the sake of completeness.

A thermal signature.

I stared at it, waiting for some transient fault to clear itself. But the signature remained. If anything, it was growing brighter, more distinct against background darkness.

I told the capsule to concentrate its sensors on that area, while it was still in view.

The image sharpened.

The thermal smudge was on a coastal inlet, exactly where we might have chosen to place a settlement. It was a harbour city, with spidering lines radiating out to more distant communities. These too were warming, beginning to glow against darkness. Lava-lines of communication and travel and energy-distribution. Hot moving sparks of vehicles, returning to the sky.

I understood.

They had dimmed their lights, turned off their power, during the period when they would have been a risk of detection, even when they were out of direct sight of the main ship. But now they thought they were safe. They were bringing their city and its surroundings out of dormancy, restarting generators, resuming normal patterns of life.

I felt puzzlement at first.

Then suspicion.

Finally a slow rising fury.

*Earth had already got here.* By some unguessable means they had come up with something faster than our Inflator Drive. While we were sleeping, they had reached Providence and settled it.

Our efforts were pointless, our noble intentions irrelevant. The people on Providence knew of our existence. They were aware of our survival, aware of our plight, and still they wished to hide their presence from us.

Not because we were a threat to them, or of any larger consequence.

I think we were an embarrassment.

We were like shabby old relatives stumbling out of the night, bringing unwanted gifts and favours. Our existence made them uncomfortable. They wanted us to go away. So they damped their fires, battened their doors, shuttered their windows and kept very, very still, pretending no one was at home.

All of which would have been theirs to know, their secret to hold, their shame to live with, except for one thing.

They had not known of me.

So, something of a dilemma.

My fury hasn't gone away. It boils in me like a hot tide, demanding release. I want to send this news back to the *Dandelion*, so that they can share in my righteous anger. That would be the proper, dutiful thing. My fellow pilgrims do not deserve to remain in ignorance about this callous, calculated act of deception.

They should learn, and know, and decide in their own time how to communicate the fact of that knowing back to Providence.

What a bitter astonishment it would be for those people on that world, to learn that their cleverness had not been sufficient. To learn that we had seen through their lie, and exposed their shame and furtiveness for what it was.

It would change no part of my fate, and make no ultimate difference to the people on the main ship. But there would be some minor solace for me in the sharing of my discovery, unburdening myself of some fraction of the anger I now carried.

So, yes, I thought long and hard about that.

In a corner of the capsule I find a dried petal.

The people on the *Dandelion* still think that they've done a good and noble thing, and I won't rob them of that. Let them continue thinking that Providence is unsettled, that their observations will wing their way back to a grateful Earth, moved to tears by their selflessness. Let them have the contentment of knowing that their information will pave the way for another expedition, that their kindness will ring down the centuries.

Let them have that.

The only snag is, I don't trust myself.

I can't let this knowledge find its way back to them. And even if rescue isn't feasible – and it probably isn't – I can't trust myself not to crack. It would be too easy to send a signal back to the *Dandelion*. At the moment my resolve feels total, unwavering. I believe I can hold a secret until my last breath.

But what I believe now, and what I'll feel when the air is guttering out, are two different things.

I'm just human, and the one thing we're not very good at is taking secrets to the grave.

I flip down the emergency panel over the pressure vent release. I settle my hand on the heavy red lever, ignoring the increasingly strident tones of the automatic warning message. I allow myself one last thought: this is also a sort of kindness, albeit not quite the one I had in mind.

And pull.

# 2001: A Space Prosthesis – The Extensions of Man

Andrew M. Butler

There is a moment in the film of *2001: A Space Odyssey* (1968) which has become one of the most famous edits in cinema: a hominid, who has seen and has been changed by a mysterious black monolith, is playing with animal bones, smashing one upon another. These have already been used as tools, including weapons. As a bone is catapulted into the air, the film leaps ahead two million years and director Stanley Kubrick matches its onscreen position to a space vehicle, probably a weapons satellite. Meanwhile, on the moon, a monolith has been discovered and this has sent a signal out into the solar system. An odyssey is set in motion.

It is overstating the case to say that tool usage distinguishes humans from animals, but no other (Earth) species has found so many ways of extending their capabilities or building civilisations. In *Civilisation and its Discontents*, Freud argues "With every tool man is perfecting his own organs, whether motor or sensory, or is removing the limits to their functioning." Glasses, telescopes, microscopes, contact lenses, telephones, television, email programs and so on extend the range of senses; cameras, records, audio cassettes, MP3s and writing preserve experiences. Cars, planes, ships, trains and spaceships allow faster travel than feet. Bows and arrows, guns, cannons and nuclear weapons allow attacks from a distance. Freud suggests that "Long ago humanity formed an ideal conception of omnipotence and omniscience which he embodied in his gods. To-day he has come very close to the attainment of this ideal, he has almost become a god himself." In *2001*, humanity achieves godlike status through the intervention of the monoliths and whatever created them. Dave Bowman – the surname is surely no accident – reaches the next stage in human evolution through his encounter with a monolith.

As extensions to or of the human, tools act as prostheses, simultaneously part of and a continuation of the human being. In Arthur C. Clarke's novel we read how the prehistoric hominid Moon-Watcher kills a pig with a stone and then uses a bone club, a knife and an awl. Such basic tools take his tribe from a subsisting group to a thriving clan, because it is easier to kill and butcher animals. They no longer starve and are better at attacking rival tribes. For some tools, there is a right side to be on and a wrong one – the killed animals and hominids are on the latter. Moon-Watcher and his kin have been uplifted by the power of the monolith, although it has to be noted that the level of violence has increased as a result of these tools.

In the book, a couple of million years later, Dr Heywood Floyd reflects upon the epochal change between implements used by European settlers of new territories and those of the "Spaceborn" who have grown up off-planet: "their tools would not be axe and gun and canoe and wagon; they would be nuclear power plant and plasma drive and hydroponic farm." Presumably, humanity has developed under its own steam after the initial stimulus of the monolith, but developed it has.

More advanced tools have been developed with the various spacesuits, rockets, space stations, space pods and *Discovery 1*, all of which allow frail bodies to travel beyond the Earth's gravity and atmosphere. Once the film has moved to the year 2001, we only see humans away from Earth, where their lives require tools – technology expands and replaces human capabilities. A crisis in *Discovery 1*'s mission occurs when Poole is cut adrift in space; Bowman retrieves the body using a pod. When such tools fail, then bodies are at risk.

The fault seems to lie with the ultimate tool, a HAL9000 computer that can monitor and control the life support systems of the *Discovery*, open and close hatches and doors remotely, facilitate communications within the ship and with Earth and does this without the need for sleep. With computers, humanity aspires to a tool that thinks. HAL has gained or been programmed with a personality – indeed, it is a commonplace of criticism that he is the most developed character in the film. The novel explains that HAL would pass the Turing Test and by any reasonable judgement is thinking, and his ability to demonstrate emotion helps enable humans to believe he is sentient. The film suggests that emotions smooth relations with humans – in other words they are tools used by a tool.

Alas, HAL has turned out to be a blunt tool. It is not clear why he fails, but the first symptom of this is when he claims the AE-35, part of the ship's radio dish, is about to fail, but Bowman and Poole can find nothing wrong with it. HAL blames human error, part of his emotional makeup being supreme confidence in his own abilities. We are repeatedly told that no HAL unit has ever failed or miscalculated, although the engineers have foreseen the need for a COMPUTER MALFUNCTION warning sign. HAL's major aim is to protect the mission – and he knows that this is not just an exploration of Jupiter (film) or Saturn (book), but a rendezvous with the destination of the signal sent by the monolith on the moon. Bowman only learns this after he has dismantled HAL's memory. HAL's actions may be a glitch in his programming, akin to trying to resolve conflicting Asimovian Laws of Robotics which demand protection of humans and itself whilst obeying orders. Reaching the signal's destination may outweigh the need to protect the crew. This does not necessarily explain his apparently mistaken diagnosis of instrument failure. As I have written, Freud saw tools as prostheses, supplementing human capabilities, but supplement has the double meaning of extension (as in dietary or newspaper supplements) and substitute. New tools make old ones obsolete. HAL's abilities make the *Discovery* crew supplementary to requirements and thus dispensable. This has deadly consequences.

Worried by this glitch, Bowman and Poole discuss whether HAL is competent to run the mission and decide to switch him off – not using a tool is safer than using a broken one. But despite their precaution of talking away from HAL's microphones, they do not realise that he is able to lip-read. HAL decides that their decision jeopardises his existence and the mission's success, and must remove the astronauts. It might be that Clarke had read D.F. Jones's *Colossus* (1960), in which a supercomputer decides that people are getting in the way of keeping the peace after it makes contact with its Soviet twin. Or Clarke might have anticipated the behaviour of the android Ash in *Alien* (1979), whose loyalty to the interests of the company that owns him outweighs his duty of care to the crew; the personnel are tools for a corporation's profit. Still, the *Discovery*'s mission to find out what it is near Jupiter/Saturn surely cannot succeed without humans to observe... aside from HAL's monitors. Their sense may be replaced. It is then that Poole is cut adrift and dies. HAL switches off life support for the three astronauts who are in deep sleep and Bowman is nearly stranded on the outside of the ship.

Bowman is able to use various kinds of equipment to outwit HAL's refusal to obey his orders, triggering explosive bolts to break back into the ship and holding his breath to survive the vacuum. He then has to use Allen keys to dismantle the ship computer. HAL loses his functions as Bowman removes each memory board, regressing to a more childlike state on his way back to basic functionality. Bowman can then use other tools – a spacesuit and a pod – to extend his life support as he has his close encounter with the monolith.

And so we came to what is the most baffling sequence of *2001*: the discovery of and journey into a monolith in space. From then on, we get a series of colours and shapes, psychedelic landscapes, with special effects technician Douglas Trumbull using his slitscreen technique to produce each visual marvel. Kubrick maintains continuity editing by cutting between this and Bowman, his eyes echoing the panoptic red eye of HAL, his helmet reflecting each strange new vision. He sees what feels like an infinite series of sublime images, an experience some of the audience allegedly heightened by the ingestion of hallucinogenic drugs to such an extent that a later poster referred to the film as "The Ultimate Trip". Such drugs are natural or artificial tools to cleanse the doors of perception and to extend humanity's vision – although like any tool there is a dark side to this.

Thanks to the novel's description of the space monolith as a Star Gate, we take the string of experiences to be a voyage into the interior of the object, although it is clearly breaking normal four-dimensional space. It could also be a voyage into the interior of Bowman, as he evolves to the next stage of humanity. We next see him as an older man in a highly decorated, Regency-style, bedroom, looking at an even older version of himself, before he becomes him, lying in the bed, gesturing towards another monolith. Finally we see a foetus, first above the bed and then – after the camera moves towards the monolith, filling the screen with black – orbiting around Earth. The Also sprach Zarathustra theme from Richard Wagner returns from earlier in the film, and the credits roll.

In the book, one of Bowman's/the Star Child's first actions is to destroy nuclear weapons in orbit around the Earth, removing one of humanity's deadlier tools: "the circling megatons flowered in a silent detonation". Here the trajectory of tool development is turned back, compared to the great span of history between hominid and spacefarer: "The spear, the bow, the gun and finally the guided missiles had given him weapons of infinite range". This addition reveals a difference between the pacifist Clarke and Kubrick: the former was optimistic about the future, the latter, having previously directed *Dr Strangelove, Or How I Learned to Stop Worrying and Love the Bomb* (1964), was anticipating Armageddon. The Moon-Watcher and Star Child (who watches the Earth) both have the same thought of wondering what to do next with their newfound abilities: "He would think of something". These lines echo the chief of the Science Bureau, Pierre Duval, in *Childhood's End* (1953), another Clarke novel in which humans are uplifted by aliens: "I will think of something."

What neither the book nor film of *2001* reveal is the nature of the aliens that have supplemented human evolution and how they benefit from this intervention. In various places in the early 1970s, Clarke records his Third Law: "Any sufficiently advanced technology is indistinguishable from magic." To Moon-Watcher, the monolith might as well be magical, for all his understanding of what is going on. As viewers of the film, the enigmas of the monoliths and the journey through the Star Gate, not to mention Bowman's eventual destination and transformation as Star Child, it might as well be magic too. All limits to his functioning have been removed. If *2001* were not located as science fiction, then we might indeed read it as fantasy. The aliens – those which we take to be behind the monoliths – are beyond our understanding. This Law has inspired several variants, including Michael Shermer's: "Any sufficiently advanced extra-terrestrial intelligence is indistinguishable from God." Indeed Clarke had suggested during the production of *2001* that "M-G-M doesn't know it yet, but they have been footing the bill for the first $10,500,000 religious film".

The monoliths are presented as teaching machines, in the book displaying images on their surface. It is tempting to wonder if, when rotated ninety degrees, the monoliths' proportions mimic the cinema screen. The film pictures teach, even as we project onto and – through identification – into the screen. *2001* across various media is another tool, extending the visions of Clarke and Kubrick around the world and beyond their deaths: a teaching machine even if the lesson itself is ambiguous.

# On Judging the Clarke Award

## Neil Gaiman

All awards are weird but some awards are weirder than others, and there was always a particular oddity to the Arthur C. Clarke Award that, in the beginning, made people talk about it and, later, made the same people respect it.

I was, for two years, an Arthur C. Clarke Award judge, and I learned then just how odd it was. For a start, as Clarke Award judges, we were sent all of the SF published in the UK in that year. Everything. And we did our best to read it all, because you never know where the undiscovered gem is hiding.

(I don't say yes to judging awards any more. I read every sf book published in the UK for two years, whether I felt like it or not, and it was only much later I found myself able to read science fiction for pleasure once again.)

The way the award worked, judges came from three different bodies: the British Science Fiction Association, the Science Fiction Foundation and, at the time, the Science Policy Foundation, with that third position currently held by the Sci-Fi-London Film Festival. Now, judging an award is difficult if you're all agreed on what it is you're judging (imagine the judges at an Olympic figure skating event, all watching for the same things), but here you had at least a couple of different criteria for excellence – imagine that one set of figure-skating judges didn't much care for the moves but would be awarding marks based on costume, or smiles, or choice of music, and then imagine the judging of the gold needed to be unanimous.

The Clarke Award was contentious: that was, frankly, part of the fun of it (the other part was the Arthur C. Clarke-donated cheque that accompanied the award), not to mention one of the reasons it was discussed in pubs and fanzines and in the proto-online communities of the time: it had been given, in its first two years, to Margaret Atwood and to George Turner, and just as the pundits had concluded that it seemed to be an award that was given to mainstream authors who had written sf, the award went to Rachel Pollack for her *Unquenchable Fire*, an uncompromising piece of magic realism, and the pundits scratched their heads and continued to argue.

It was about this point that I noticed that the Arthur C. Clarke Award was being taken seriously – or as seriously as sf awards are taken. It occupied its own unique niche, and now, after over thirty years, it is still in its own niche.

My own Clarke Award judging experiences, over two years, were about as different as they could possibly have been. In one of the years blood was spilled, horses were traded, and the judges faced off and fought for their books, each judge having a completely different idea of what the award was, what kind of book it should be given to, what kind of shortlist they wanted to see, what kind of book should ultimately win. In the other year an IRA bomb threat made it impossible for half the judges to get to the shortlist judging, and made for a very easy and quiet judging process for those who were there. Looking back at the books that won, I'm satisfied with both of them, not least because neither of them was like any other book that had won.

Honestly, I think it's probably a good thing to have at least a couple of the judges looking at the figure skaters quite differently to their fellows, because the Clarke Award is, I suspect, ultimately about bridge-building, which may be one reason why it is, although a British award, recognised and respected internationally. The Arthur C. Clarke Award is the award that the world of sf offers, each year, to the world outside as an example of both what sf is and what it can be.

The perfect Arthur C. Clarke Award winner has little in common with any of the other winners except, perhaps, that in the places where people gather together to argue, a Clarke shortlist and a Clarke winner will give them plenty to talk about.

# Once More on the 3rd Law

## China Miéville

Arthur C Clarke was a fearsomely quotable man.

'Sometimes I think we're alone in the universe, and sometimes I think we're not. In either case the idea is quite staggering.' More than a cosmological one, this is an existential observation. Rarely has the inevitability of awe been so precisely invoked. The legendary last line of 'The Nine Billion Names of God' – 'Overhead, without any fuss, the stars were going out.' – deserves its canonical place, but it is the penultimate line that most sears: '(There is always a last time for everything.)' We stand in mute gratitude for its precision, dignity of its mourning, the courage to deploy parentheses that tug the sentence from the story, a pre-emptive elegy and a statement of fact.

Of his various saws, apophthegms and aperçus, Clarke's most famous is his Third Law. It is so well-known that it suffers from the contempt of familiarity (*Any sufficiently advanced blah blah blah is indistinguishable yadda yadda yadda*). Once more, then, with feeling and with thought: 'Any sufficiently advanced technology is indistinguishable from magic.'

The claim is historical and social, epistemological, and – slyly, and of most concern to us here – literary. It is a consummate provocation. On its foolishness and/or its wisdom, takes, hot and not, outraged and temperate, abound. Not least because it is clever, back-handed compliment to the author's literary genre, the field this very book celebrates. 'Magic', after all, means wondrous. But it means other things too. Spoken in a certain tone, the word has, for example, an end-of-the-pier quality, a faintly shabby prestidigitatory implication: all quick fingers, questionable props, wool pulled over eyes. *Trickery.* The Law doesn't claim that advanced tech and magic are identical... but to be truly 'indistinguishable', they might be. And that, particularly for a field of fiction committed to dreams of conceptual rigour, is, in the final analysis, an insult. The Third Law, as many commentators note in glee or anguish, would eradicate any fundamental break between the genres of science fiction and fantasy.

This is, of course, a hoary issue, and one over which border guards have invested much energy. For years, critics proposed a Rubicon between the literatures, on grounds of rigour versus rigourlessness, potentiality versus impossibility of the unreals they propose as true – the specifically 'cognitive estrangement' of science fiction, in the words of the seminal theorist of the division, and of sf *tout court*, Darko Suvin. And that divide, very often, they made vertical, qualitative - almost always to the detriment of fantasy.

Let the record reflect that Suvin latterly revisited, problematised, and substantially nuanced his earlier claim that fantasy was 'a sub-literature of mystification'. This shift reflected and encouraged a growing scepticism about the border wall. That there are bundles of norms, paraphernalia of form and content, let alone of marketing strategies distinguishing the two great pulp wings of non-realist fiction, is not in doubt. Let the debates continue. But there are growing numbers of us for whom the idea that these express an underlying philosophical schism, let alone hierarchy, is quite unconvincing.

In those it has honoured, the Clarke Award itself, of course, has form in cheerfully ignoring any such split. So there is something appropriate and winning, deeply charming, in the fact that Clarke himself, this most establishment, most 'traditional', scientifically trained, science-friendly of science fiction writers off-handedly interpenetrated the two fields, that he did so so early, that he did so with humour. That, whether he reflected on the fact or not, he set up a dissenting theory of fiction.

This is a model that doesn't flip but undermines binaries. The point is not that there's no 'real' 'rationalism' in science fiction (henceforth, thickets of scare quotes unavoidably thrive). Rather, it is that in various degrees and kinds, to variegated ends, varyingly vividly, what characterises the tradition is oscillation, a generative tension between those tendencies synecdoched in 'technology' and 'magic'. Science and religion, maths and vision. Rationalism and the sublime. Engineering and ecstasy.

It has long been clear that Clarke is exemplary of this relation: two decades ago, in the *New York Times*, Gary Wolfe described his 'paradoxical dual identity as rationalist and mystic'. And Clarke is not alone. Often it does not know it, but even the scienciest of science fiction is a literature of tension. Of the sayable and the unsayable. This is no criticism: it is what makes it, at its best, so remarkable – heir of Edison, yes, and of Hildegarde of Bingen, too. This is the anxiety of the field, and its glory.

Which is not any guarantor of quality. There is not nor will there ever be any shortage of dreadful sf produced. But we read and write in, on one axis at least, an exciting moment: these days the snobbery against sf *qua* literature has arguably less traction than it ever has. Holdouts dig in to their literary trenches, of course, but there has never been a moment when the science-fictional is as ascendant – not merely at the pop-cultural level (with which of course there is nothing wrong) but at the *haute*.

This shift is a relief in part because the outraged defences from genre's partisans, and our complaints that 'the mainstream' 'disrespectfully' 'steals' 'our' 'ideas', have, justness notwithstanding, long been no less dull than the attacks of highbrow trolls themselves. (Now, if anything, in the rubble of geek triumph, as the engines of the culture industry spin with their usual remorseless energy to exude mediocrity for our enthusiastic consumption, we might perhaps consider that on the whole it is we who are failing respectfully to pilfer enough from the mainstream.)

Here, though, let us set grumpy-old-codgerism aside. More and more readers can now agree, as Clarke Award-watchers have long known, that any sufficiently advanced science fiction is indistinguishable from literature.

One popular, bad argument that often follows is that there should be no distinctions at all made in fiction (except perhaps, it may winsomely be added, between good fiction and bad). To hierarchies of genre, good riddance indeed. But this model leaves out questions of specificities, the fact that not all literature does whatever strange things it does with the same attentions or tools or in the same way.

Culturally, we like the sort of things we like more than we like the sort of things we don't like as much, and from the inevitable fact that we will struggle to articulate the borders of those sets – grey areas will be very large and very grey – it doesn't follow that they are not sorts of things at all.

There are specificities to aesthetics. There are distinctions. One of the most pertinent and pregnant, to which it is impossible not to return, is that between two ways of relating to the world. Call them recognition and estrangement – or, as Sarah Crown vividly described them, literature 'of the "ah yes!" variety' and of the '"oh, my" sort'.

All fiction, all art, contains elements of both, in complex imbrication. Without recognition, there is no way in: without any estrangement from givens, this is not art. Such drives are inextricable, mutually constituted, and sometimes work in very close tandem. When, a century ago, Viktor Shklovsky argued for defamiliarisation, that art should 'make objects "unfamiliar"', it could be construed as the deployment of estrangement for the very end of sharpening recognition. But there is, too, always-already a tension; a question, even if unanswerable, of which ultimately underlies the other; a sense in which in their jostling and overlap, they do not only depict but know the world as knowable or unknowable. As much as it *makes* strange, estrangement *acknowledges* a fundamental strangeness. The balance and the tension between these two make for different literatures.

In science fiction, in the fantastic more generally, the depiction of impossibilities-as-real is key to the estranging drive. For all the clichés and failures of imagination of much sf, its readers and writers tend, more than for the 'ah yes', to beg to beg for the 'oh my'.

There need be no hierarchy. Those who want from art to be shown things that they know but have, perhaps, not expressed or conceived with such exactitude, have every right to it. There is intense pleasure in it. Even illumination. The yearning for such moments should not be gainsaid, any more than should the urges of those for whom that other kind of rigour is key. Those who seek the epiphany of alterity.

(Though might matters in fact go further than that? Might we dignify our sf-inflected otherness-hankerings as of qualitative significance? Some of us share an intuition that at its best there is something particular and distinctly important about the art of otherness. Art that sits uneasy. That estranges. That, to appropriate from Walter Benjamin, rubs history against the grain. Because of course, yes, this is in part, broadly, about the politics of art – which, we add in weary caveat, need not mean that in a prescriptive or sectarian way; nor be about the politics of the artist, still less reading off artistic quality therefrom; nor imply that self-styled 'radical' or 'political' art will necessarily perform its work, including the estranging work, successfully. But we digress.)

We who for whom, with all honour to recognition, estrangement is key, need not pretend otherwise. And even if we hesitate to ascribe greater importance to the estranging drive than to its obverse, or to address utopian questions of politics and form, the model of the dyad justifies itself in various ways. Not least, it clarifies certain evasive facts about literature itself.

Affective response – a hunch, even – matters. *Jane Eyre*; *Moby Dick*; *Heart of Darkness*; *Attic Summer*. What do we make of such books, a sub-tradition of literature which contains *no* explicitly unreal, fantastic content, and yet which the lover of the weird, the science-fictional, reads as of a piece with the rest of their favoured canon? As if these, too, were such fabular works? Surely that it is the underlying estrangement which pulls us in. That though the fantastic content is one common way to articulate that, it is not the only one, and that the effect can be achieved, quite brilliantly, in its absence.

For years, we on the gutter-side of literature kvetched lengthily and moaned, hankered for a day when fantastic work won major book awards. Had we retained any lingering doubt that we have reached it, the fact that the most recent winner of the Clarke Award, Colson Whitehead's *The Underground Railroad*, also took the Pulitzer and National Book Award should dispense with it.

We, to put it another way, won.

So what is there yet to long for?

A new and final confidence, is what. A paradoxical reflection of that triumph. A day when our confidence and joy in our tradition of estrangement, in its pulp iterations and in others, means that the Arthur C Clarke Award honours such a book, one without a single explicit unreal, fantastic element. One of those rare but wonderful works that, in the strangeness of its depicted real, it shakes up the everyday, radically estranges, reconfiguring the world. What else could one want from a winner?

When among the generation starships and the wormholes and the aliens we love, a work of such a-realism is the best of its estranging kind that year, as if nothing else chance would dictate that sometimes it must be, let it win. Even once. If such a book were announced the best science fiction of the year, that need not herald the end of the sf tradition but its triumph. We need not be scared.

Any sufficiently advanced science fiction is indistinguishable from literature, indeed. That should not ever have been controversial. But we can go further, honouring the tradition we love with its own strange sublation. Starting from a preference for the literature of estrangement, this last move remains controversial (even though *we did this already* (*Quicksilver*, Neil Stephenson, 2004)). It is, though, profoundly exciting to consider that any sufficiently advanced literature must be indistinguishable from science fiction.

# About the Authors

**Matthew De Abaitua**'s debut novel *The Red Men* was shortlisted for the Arthur C Clarke Award and published in the US for the first time in November 2017. His science fiction novels *IF THEN* (Angry Robot, 2015) and *The Destructives* (Angry Robot, 2016) were described as "Extraordinary visionary... the most intriguing and disturbing near-future speculations published for some years." (Andy Sawyer, Strange Horizons).

His latest book is *Self & I: A Memoir of Literary Ambition* (Eye Books, 2018) about his time as Will Self's amanuensis in the 1990s. He lectures on creative writing and science fiction at the University of Essex and lives in Hackney.

**Chris Beckett** published his first short story in *Interzone* in 1990. He is the author of six novels and three short story collections. His novel *Dark Eden* won the Arthur C. Clarke award in 2012. His short story collection, *The Turing Test*, won the Edge Hill Prize in 2009. His most recent novel is *America City*. His new short story collection, *Spring Tide*, was published in Jan 2018. A former social worker and social work lecturer, Chris lives in Cambridge. More information at www.chris-beckett.com

**Becky Chambers** is the author of the *Wayfarers* books, which currently include *The Long Way to a Small, Angry Planet, A Closed and Common Orbit*, and *Record of a Spaceborn Few*. Her work has been nominated for the Hugo Award, the Arthur C. Clarke Award, and the Bailey's Women's Prize for Fiction, among others. She also writes essays and short stories.

In addition to writing, Becky has a background in performing arts, and grew up in a family heavily involved in space science. She spends her free time playing video and tabletop games, fussing with her telescope, and stomping around the woods. Having hung her hat in Scotland and Iceland, she's now back in her home state of California, where she lives with her wife and about a hundred thousand honeybees.

**Neil Gaiman** is an author of short fiction, novels, comic books, graphic novels, audio theatre, and films. His notable works include the comic book series *The Sandman* and novels *Stardust, American Gods, Coraline*, and *The Graveyard Book*. He has won numerous awards, including the Hugo, Nebula, and Bram Stoker, as well as the Newbery and Carnegie medals. He is the first author to win both the Newbery and the Carnegie medals for the same work, *The Graveyard Book* (2008). In 2013, *The Ocean at the End of the Lane* was voted Book of the Year in the British National Book Awards.

In 1990, **Colin Greenland** became the first British author to win the Arthur C. Clarke Award, with *Take Back Plenty*, his fourth published novel and the first volume of the Tabitha Jute trilogy. He is still writing, fitfully, some of it even science fiction, though "Before They Left" is the first thing he's had published for ages. It's an extra chapter for *Childhood's End*, he says, which Arthur never got around to writing.

**Stephanie Holman** is a director of the Serendip Foundation, the governing body of the Arthur C. Clarke Award, and is currently completing a BA in Creative Writing. She is passionate about science fiction film from *2001: A Space Odyssey* to *Arrival* and has a mild addiction to Secret Cinema screenings.

**Tom Hunter** is the director of the Arthur C. Clarke Award, the UK's premier prize for science fiction literature. He works in marketing and has always been carefully to avoid an actual career in publishing lest it forever ruin his love for books. That said, since first taking on the Clarke Award challenge over a decade ago he has been actively involved in promoting science fiction at every opportunity, including writing, reviewing, public speaking, coaching, lots and lots of author interviews, and even organising his own conference event, Write The Future (WTF). This anthology represents a chance to say a huge thank you to the memory of Sir Arthur for all of those opportunities, past, present and, of course, future.

**Dave Hutchinson** was born in Sheffield in 1960 and read American Studies at the University of Nottingham before becoming a journalist. He is the author of four novels, two novellas, and five collections of short stories. His novella "The Push" was nominated for the BSFA Award in 2010, and the volumes of his Fractured Europe Sequence of novels have been nominated for the Arthur C. Clarke, BSFA, Kitschies and John W. Campbell Memorial awards. The third novel, *Europe in Winter*, won the BSFA Award in 2017. He lives in London.

**Emmi Itäranta** (born 1976) grew up in Finland and now resides in Canterbury, UK. She writes fiction in Finnish and English. Her debut novel *Memory of Water* (HarperVoyager 2014) has won numerous awards, including a James Tiptree Jr. Award honours list mention and the Kalevi Jäntti Prize for young writers in Finland. It was nominated for the Philip K. Dick Award, Arthur C. Clarke Award, the Kitschies Golden Tentacle Award, the Compton Crook Award and Premio Salerno Libro d'Europa. Emmi's second novel, *The*

*City of Woven Streets* (UK) / *The Weaver* (US) won the Tampere City Literary Award and the Kuvastaja Award for the best fantasy book in Finland.

Coming from an eclectic writing background, Emmi's former life includes stints as a columnist, theatre critic, dramaturge, scriptwriter and press officer. She wishes to keep writing until the stars go cold. You can find her online at www.emmiitaranta.com.

**Gwyneth Jones** is a writer and critic of genre fiction, who has also written for teenagers using the name Ann Halam. She's won a few awards, but doesn't let it get her down. She lives in Brighton, UK, with her husband and two cats called Milo and Tilly, curating assorted pondlife in season. She's a member of the Soil Association, the Sussex Wildlife Trust, Frack Free Sussex and the Green Party; and an Amnesty International volunteer. Hobbies include watching old movies, playing Zelda and staring out of the window.

**Yoon Ha Lee**'s debut novel *Ninefox Gambit* won the Locus Award for best first novel and was a finalist for the Clarke, Hugo, and Nebula awards. He lives in Louisiana with his family and a lazy cat, and has not yet been eaten by gators.

**Ian R. Macleod** is the author of seven novels and five short story collections. His work has been widely translated and anthologised and, as well as receiving the Arthur C Clarke Award for his novel *Song of Time*, has been the recipient and nominee for most of the major gene awards. He lives in the riverside town of Bewdley. He says he was very much aware of Clarke's "The Ten Billion Names of God" when he came up with the rough idea for this story, which he read with admiration, and not a little awe, while on an otherwise rather miserable school geography field trip when he was 14.

**Phillip Mann** was born in North Yorkshire. After working in drama in the USA, he moved to New Zealand where, apart from working in the theatre, he founded the first New Zealand Drama Studies Department at Victoria University. He began writing Science Fiction while working at the New China News Agency in Beijing. To date he has published ten Science Fiction novels as well as many short stories, articles etc. His novel, *The Disestablishment of Paradise* was a finalist for the Arthur C. Clarke Award in 2014. Further information on his writing can be found on his web page at Phillipmann.co.nz

**Paul McAuley** worked as a research biologist and university lecturer before becoming a full-time writer. He is the author of more than twenty novels, several collections of short stories, a Doctor Who novella, and a BFI Film Classic monograph on Terry Gilliam's film *Brazil*. His fiction has won the

Philip K Dick Memorial Award, the Arthur C. Clarke Award, the John W. Campbell Memorial Award, the Sidewise Award, the British Fantasy Award and the Theodore Sturgeon Memorial Award. His latest novel, *Austral*, a novel about post-global warming Antarctica, was published in 2017.

**Ian McDonald** is a science fiction (mostly) writer living in Northern Ireland, just outside Belfast. His first novel, *Desolation Road*, was published in 1988, his most recent is *Luna: Wolf Moon*, the second part of the Luna series. Forthcoming in *Luna: Moon Rising*. He's been nominated for every major SFF award and even won a few. His work has been translated into seventeen languages. After working for many years in television, he's quit the Sisyphean task of trying to devise new formats for antique shows and has returned to the peace and satisfaction of writing full time.

**China Miéville** is a fantasy fiction author, comic writer, political activist and academic. His work has won numerous awards, including the Arthur C. Clarke Award (three times), the British Fantasy Award (twice), the Locus Award for Best Fantasy Novel (four times) and Best Science Fiction Novel, Locus Awards for Best Novelette and Best Young Adult Books, as well as the Hugo, Kitschies and World Fantasy Awards. His novel *The City and the City* was adapted into an ambitious four-part series televised by the BBC in 2018.

**Emma Newman** writes short stories, novels and novellas in multiple speculative fiction genres. She won the British Fantasy Society Best Short Story Award 2015 for "A Woman's Place" in the *Two Hundred and Twenty-One Baker Streets* anthology. Her science-fiction novel, *After Atlas*, was shortlisted for the 2017 Arthur C. Clarke Award. Emma is an audiobook narrator and also co-writes and hosts the Hugo and Alfie Award winning podcast "Tea and Jeopardy". Her hobbies include LARP, tabletop RPGs and dressmaking. She blogs at www.enewman.co.uk and can be found as @emapocalyptic on Twitter.

**Jeff Noon** was born in Manchester, England. He trained in the visual arts and drama and was active on the post-punk music scene before becoming a playwright, and then a novelist. His novels include *Vurt* (Arthur C. Clarke Award winner), *Pollen, Automated Alice, Nymphomation, Needle in the Groove, Cobralingus, Falling Out Of Cars, Channel SK1N, Mappalujo* (with Steve Beard), *A Man of Shadows* and a collection of stories called *Pixel Juice*. He has also won the John W. Campbell Award. His latest novel is *The Body Library*, published by Angry Robot in 2018.

**Claire North** is a pseudonym for Catherine Webb, who also writes as Kate Griffin. Her first book published as Claire North was *The First Fifteen Lives of Harry August*, which was shortlisted for the Arthur C. Clarke Award. *The Sudden Appearance of Hope* won the 2017 World Fantasy Award for Best Novel, and *The End of the Day* was shortlisted for the 2017 Sunday Times/PFD Young Writer of the Year Award. Her latest book is *84K*, published spring 2018. Claire works as a lighting designer and loves big cities, Thai food and graffiti-spotting. She lives in London.

**Rachel Pollack** is the author of forty books of fiction and non-fiction, including the award-winning novels, *Unquenchable Fire* and *Godmother Night*, as well as a series of books about Tarot cards that have earned her the title of "Tazot Grandmaster." Her books have been translated into 15 languages, and sold all across the world. Her most recent book is *The fissure King – A Novel In Five Stories*.

**Alastair Reynolds** was born in Barry, South Wales, where he encountered his first Arthur C Clarke story a week after his eighth birthday. He went on to study space science, and eventually worked for the European Space Agency in the Netherlands. He started writing science fiction not long after that birthday but took a little longer to get into print. He is now the author of sixteen novels and more than seventy short stories, of which his most recent book is Elysium Fire. He returned to Wales in 2008.

**Adam Roberts** is a university academic and writer of science fiction who lives a little way west of London. His most recent book is *The Real-Town Murders* (Gollancz). The first Arthur C Clarke book he read was *A Fall of Moondust* when he was ten years old. He's now more than five times that age, and has read everything Clarke published

**Jane Rogers** is an award-winning novelist, short story writer, and radio dramatist. She is author of nine novels, including *The Testament of Jessie Lamb*, Man-Booker longlisted and winner of the Arthur C Clarke Award 2012. Other works include *Mr Wroe's Virgins* (which she dramatised for the BAFTA-nominated BBC drama series), *Her Living Image* (Somerset Maugham Award) and *Promised Lands* (Writers Guild Best Fiction Award). She has written original drama for Radio 4, and adapted numerous novels for the *Classic Serial* slot.

Jane is Emerita Professor of Writing at Sheffield Hallam, and a Fellow of the Royal Society of Literature. She teaches Short Story for Faber Academy, and is currently working on a new science fiction novel. Find her online at: www.janerogers.info

**Bruce Sterling**, author, journalist, editor, and critic, is best known for his ten science fiction novels, including the Arthur C. Clarke Award winner *Distraction*, though he also writes short stories, book reviews, design criticism, opinion columns, introductions, and nonfiction. His most recent book is a collection of Italian fantascienza stories, *Utopia Pirata: I Racconti Di Bruno Argento* (2016). In 2016 he was Visionary in Residence at the Arthur C. Clarke Center for Human Imagination. He has appeared on TV in both the USA and the UK, and featured in publications including *Time, Newsweek, The Wall Street Journal, the New York Times, Fortune, Nature, I.D., Metropolis, Technology Review, Der Spiegel, La Stampa, La Repubblica*, and many other venues. He unites his time among the cities of Austin, Turin and Belgrade.

**Allen Stroud** (Ph. D) is a Science Fiction, Fantasy and Horror writer, best known for his work on the computer game Elite Dangerous and its official fiction. His latest book, *The Forever Man*, was published in 2017 by Luna Press. Allen is editor of the *British Fantasy Society Journal* and co-lead writer for Phoenix Point, a computer game coming out in 2018. You can find more of Allen's Phoenix Point stories here: https://phoenixpoint.info/archives/
He is also Chair of Fantasycon 2018.

**Adrian Tchaikovsky** was born in Lincolnshire and lives in Leeds. He is a keen role-player, aspiring entomologist and former amateur actor, as well as a student of historical combat. He has written fifteen novels including the Shadows of the Apt and Echoes of the Fall series, *Guns of the Dawn, Spiderlight* and the recent SF works *Children of Time* and *Dogs of War*. He won the Arthur C Clarke award in 2016 and the British Fantasy Award in 2017.

**Ian Watson** is noted for his screen story for the movie *A.I. Artificial Intelligence* (2001) directed by Steven Spielberg after the death of Stanley Kubrick – with whom Ian worked on that project eyeball to eyeball throughout 1990. Ian watched Kubrick's film *2001: A Space Odyssey* in 1970 in a Tokyo cinema in a bucket seat which was a real squeeze compared with Kubrick and Clarke's spacious spaceship *Discovery One* on the way to Jupiter. As regards SF, Ian was first bowled over as a schoolboy by the British Pan Books paperback of Clarke's *Childhood's End*, 1956, price two shillings, and in 2001 Ian almost co-edited with Arthur *The Lost Worlds of A.I.* but this book was not to be.

**Ian Whates** was a judge of the Arthur C. Clarke Award in 2014 and 2016. He is the author of seven novels (four space opera and three urban fantasy with steampunk overtones), the co-author of two more (military SF), has seen some seventy of his short stories published in a variety of venues, and has edited around thirty anthologies. His work has been shortlisted for the Philip K. Dick

Award and twice for BSFA Awards and has been translated into Spanish, German, Hungarian, Czech and Greek. In 2006 he founded award-winning independent publisher NewCon Press by accident and continues to be baffled by the number of titles the imprint has produced.

**Liz Williams** writes science fiction and dark fantasy. Her novels have been published by Bantam Spectra and Night Shade Press in the USA and by Tor Macmillan in the UK. Four of her novels have been nominated for the Philip K. Dick Award, and *Banner Of Souls* was also nominated for the Arthur C. Clarke Award. She has appeared regularly on the *New York Times'* Best of Year lists. She has published over eighty short stories, many of which have been awarded Honourable Mention or been published in the *Best of Year* collections. She is secretary of the long-running Milford SF Writers' Workshop, and has also written travel pieces for the *Rough Guide*. She is currently writing a non-fiction history of British paganism.

# Supporters List

The editors and publisher would like to acknowledge the following people for their support in ensuring this project came into being:

David Tubby
Steve Walsh
Ed R
James Hewison-Carter
Tomoyuki Hirao
Joerg Mueller-Kindt
Andrew Clark
Foruli
Keith Prochaska
Tom Loock
Mark Slater
Jason Guth
René Rasmussen
A.G. Carter
Andrew Hatchell
Mark Pitman
Andrew Ferguson
Jon Storey
Jaromir Dukaczewski
Stephen Barr
Christian Schellenberger
Iain McKay
Stephen
Rodney O'Connor
Duncan Lawie
Chris Brooks
F. D. Lee
S. Naomi Scott
Craig D Hewitt
Mike Griffiths
Jim Cairl
Stephen Booth
Karel Šec
Joost Landgraf

James Goddard
Neal Chuang
Robert R Thompson
Tim Sherburn
Ian Chung
Aaron Morris
William R. Edgington
Steve Hurowitz
Nick Hubble
Ross Loveland
Jackie Coleman
Mark Hood
Shield Bonnichsen
Maria Lehtman
Sam Barillaro
Sachin Suchak
Brian Parker
Michael Hirtzy
Richard Crowe
Jan-Henrik Wilhelm
Chris Petrella
Danny Dyer
Rosie Boughton
Peter Gleeson
Kathryn Hunter
Ian Watson
Andy Theyers
Adam Bowie
Martin McGrath
Michael Flett
Finbarr Farragher
Anthony Perrett
Melani Weber
A.B.

Pete Randall
Stuart James Mackenzie
Leonardo Salvatore
Claire Sims
Roger Robinson
Lee W. Pfahler
Daniel Hickie Dugdale
Kotaro Kawaguchi
Marcus Gipps
Steve Crisp
Lucius M. Nelligan Sorrentino
Paul Saxon-Shaw
E.M. Middel
Mike Calder
Martin Helsdon
Steve Barnett
Adrian Hickford
Amy Griffiths
Sergio Fraile Carmena
Niall Gordon
Ardis L. Ramey
Guy Trott
Clay K. S. Walton
Tony Lee
Alan & Julyan Hunter
Steve Dunn
Dave M. Roberts
Bernadette Lewis
Jeb Weisman
Chris Drakiotes
Richard Libera
Paul David Blizzard
Dino Drakiotes
Adam Hall
Graeme Strachan
Juan R. Soto Rosa
David Michael Anderson
Paul M. Feeney
Duncan MacGregor
Byran Caleb Segers

Abhilash Sarhadi
Tokzer
Dominique Martel
Andy Leighton
Linda White
Mark T Croucher
Simon Bradshaw
Chris Girdlestone
Patrick Rogers
Caroline Mersey
Mike Moore
Christina Woelke
Michael Brookes
Matthew Lavin
Björn Johansson
Jasmine Karim
Chris 'HFO' Harris
Tm O-The
Matt Hill
Mark Clerkin
Yacoob Al-Atawi
Hennie Gottenbos
Richard H.
John Squire
John Hunter
Gerard Earley
Pascal Desbarats
Dave Smith
Diane Severson Mori
Jo
Gavin Pugh
Steph Parker
Cecilia Weightman
Neil Currie
Richard Ashcroft
Tero Ykspetäjä
Y. K. Lee
Carol Goodwin
Molly Flatt
Terry Somerville

Tibs
Nick Tyler
Radoslaw Kot
Chris Cowan
Kevin Hendeson
Tarek A. Hijaz
Jordan D.W. Smith
Martin McCallion
John Jarrold
Jon Callas
Patrik R. Maass
Ray Street
Jakob S. Pfafferodt
Stephanie Lucas
Daniel M. Clark
Jim Bassett
Matt Webb
Alan Andrews
Y. Levy
Talkie Tim
Wendy Rogers
Gregory Sharp
Alan Millard
Andrew Curry
Simon Lydiard FRSA
Claire Margerison
Henry Burrows
Phil Barrett
Georgie Knight

Kevin J. "Womzilla" Maroney
Richard Scott
Alison Southern
Michael P
David Jessop
Sally Novak Janin
SFBook
Reiley Lees
Annabel Grundy
Sam Brady
Matt Gordon
Andrew Linke
Russ Smith
Doug Finazzi
April Brewer
Rishikesh Mehta
Paul 'Barking Pumpkin' Spence
Jeffrey Graebner
Clinton Kindle
Tom Potts
Stefan Brinkman
Martin Bernstein
York Science Fiction Book Club
Adam Osborne
Craig Poole
Dagmar Baumann
Lindsay Fursland
Elliott Fin

# Fables From The Fountain
### Homage to Arthur C. Clarke's classic
## Tales from the White Hart

**The Fountain**: a traditional London pub situated in Holborn, just off Chancery Lane, where Michael, the landlord, serves excellent real ales and dodgy ploughman's, ably assisted by barmaids Sally and Bogna.

**The Fountain**, in whose Paradise Bar Prof Macintosh, Crown Baker, 'Tweet' Peston, Dr. Steve, Jocelyn Sparrow, Ray Arnold, Laura Fowler, Brian Dalton and their friends – scientists, writers and science fiction readers – meet on a Tuesday night to swap anecdotes, reveal wondrous events from their past, tell tall tales, talk of classified invention and, maybe, just maybe, save the world…

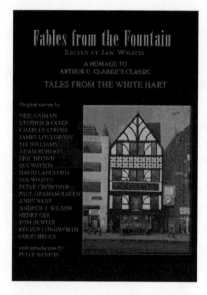

With original stories by:

**Neil Gaiman**
**Stephen Baxter**
**Charles Stross**
**Adam Roberts**
**Liz Williams**
**Eric Brown**
**James Lovegrove**
**Ian Watson**
**David Langford**
**Peter Crowther**
**Ian Whates**
**Andy West**
**Tom Hunter**
**Paul Graham Raven**
**Andrew J. Wilson**
**Henry Gee**
And more…

Originally published in 2011, Fables has been out of print for some years. NewCon Press are delighted to announce the release of a second edition of the book, which acts as a fundraiser for the Arthur C. Clarke Award.

http://www.newconpress.co.uk